Remember Our Yesterdays

REMEMBER OUR YESTERDAYS

□

C. V. BOECKMAN

AVALON BOOKS
THOMAS BOUREGY AND COMPANY, INC.
401 LAFAYETTE STREET
NEW YORK, NEW YORK 10003

PRINTED IN THE UNITED STATES OF AMERICA
ON ACID-FREE PAPER
BY HADDON CRAFTSMEN, SCRANTON, PENNSYLVANIA

For my daughter, Sharla

Chapter One

I'd had a couple of routine jobs earlier that week, serving some legal papers and helping locate a guy who was behind on his child-support payments. That's the kind of work that keeps a female private investigator in business. The glamorous chase scenes look swell on TV, but they don't happen much to real-life private detectives. It's a good thing; my battered old Ford pickup would fall to pieces if I ever pushed it much over sixty.

I also do some investigative jobs for insurance companies and law firms, although finding missing persons is my speciality.

By Wednesday, I'd served the papers and located the rat who was ducking child support, and then I was reduced to sitting at my desk doing paperwork, which I hate. Times like that, I wished my job was a little more like those of the private eyes on TV. Those guys all have secretaries. Of course, they also get shot at a lot.

It was late Wednesday when my office door opened and

in walked six feet of tall, lanky Texan appropriately attired in boots, jeans, and elaborately stitched shirt. He was wearing a black Stetson, which, in true drugstore-cowboy style, he did not remove. (I think they wear them to bed.) At second glance, I saw this was no run-of-the-mill drugstore cowboy getup. The alligator boots probably cost five hundred dollars at a custom boot shop. The ornate shirt had real topaz-and-sterling-silver decorations. And the rubies and diamonds that encrusted his wide gold buckle looked real, not to mention the gold itself. After my eyes had adjusted to all that opulent glare, I got a closer look at his face and saw a drooping black mustache, bushy black eyebrows, and a tan that I suspected came more from a tanning salon than riding the range.

I stared at him, wondering where I'd seen him before.

"K. R. McHaney?" he asked.

When new clients walk in, they usually think I'm the secretary and K. R. McHaney must be a six-foot guy chomping on a cigar in a back room somewhere. But this client had his piercing jet-black eyes fixed on me, and they didn't blink when I acknowledged that I was the K. R. McHaney whose name was spelled out on the frosted-glass panel in my office door. (The "K" stands for Kate.)

"I'm Freddie Landers," he said.

That rang a bell. Now I knew why he looked familiar. Freddie Landers was a local country-western, rock and roll bandleader. Until a few years ago, he'd performed around the Rio Grande valley and up and down the border in honky-tonks, strictly small-time, third-rate, and unknown. Then he wrote "Remember Our Yesterdays."

A local studio recorded the song, and a disc jockey in a valley radio station gave it some play. It became an instant hit locally. Other stations picked it up. Before you could say Johnny Cash, "Remember Our Yesterdays" was in the top forty and climbing to the top of the charts. It brought Freddie Landers national fame and fortune. And it wasn't a flash in the pan. Freddie followed up his first hit with "Your Head on My Pillow," "Long Gone from Here," and "Used to Your Lovin'," all of them top forty, two of them platinum sellers. The songs got Freddie Las Vegas bookings, concert tours, and exposure on a nationally syndicated TV country-western show. They also made him a very wealthy man. He hadn't had a hit song in a while, but he didn't need it.

Freddie kept his home base here in the Rio Grande valley of south Texas. But he no longer lived in a run-down trailer park. These days he hung his cowboy hat in a sprawling, palatial ranch-style home with a swimming pool shaped like a guitar. He owned various businesses around the valley: citrus fruit groves, a foreign sports car dealership, a music store. He was also involved in a big land deal to build a Freddie Landers country-western theme park. The latest thing I'd heard about him was that a motion-picture producer out of Dallas was down here, shooting a low-budget movie about Freddie's life and music, *The Freddie Landers Story*.

So I had a nationally known celebrity in my modest office. "Yes," I said. "I know who you are."

He took a seat facing my desk, pushed his Western hat back with a forefinger, and stared at me. For what seemed a number of seconds we just stared at each other. Maybe he was sizing me up; I don't know. As for myself, I was going through some mental gymnastics, pictures flashing through my mind of TV and tabloid images of Freddie Landers superimposed on the real thing seated a few feet away. I'd read somewhere that he was in his mid-twenties. Without the makeup, he looked a bit more tired and dissipated, but otherwise much the same as on TV.

I toyed with the idea of asking for his autograph, but decided on a more professional approach. "What can I do for you, Mr. Landers?"

"Is it okay if I smoke?"

I agreed that it was and from a gold case he removed one of those long, skinny, black cheroots you see in Western movies and touched a flame to it from a lighter that I was not surprised to see was also gold. That was when I noticed that his hands were shaking.

Once he had the thin cigar lighted, he stared down at it as if it contained the secrets of the universe. After some long moments, he pulled his consciousness back to the matter at hand, drew a deep breath, and said, "I want to hire you to do some investigating for me."

"What kind of investigating, Mr. Landers?"

He didn't answer immediately. He paid some attention to his cigar again for a bit, then asked about my rates. I explained my policy about an advance against my hourly rate plus expenses. I had the feeling he wasn't even listening.

He said, "I asked around. They tell me you're very good. I think a woman investigator would be better at what I need. Certain people might get suspicious if a strange man started poking around." He nodded as if he had been convincing himself. "You could come over to my house tomorrow. I'm throwing a big fiesta. Everybody will be there—business associates, the motion-picture people, friends, relatives. I could tell them you're a second cousin from Laredo. That way, you could get a handle on who they are and check them out."

"Just what am I supposed to be checking out, Mr. Landers?"

He had a peculiar expression as he looked at me. His hand was shaking badly as he snuffed out his cigar in an ashtray on my desk. "Somebody is trying to kill me. I want you to find out who it is."

Chapter Two

I felt the hair prickle on the back of my neck. "Now, wait a minute, Mr. Landers. If you suspect somebody is out to murder you, you don't need my services. You need to go to the police."

"I've been to the police," he said with a worried frown. "They want to know who's been making threats. What can I say? Nobody's come right out and threatened me. I don't have anything that definite. They said they'd check into it, but what they were really doing was giving me the brush-off. They figure people like me in the music business smoke funny cigarettes, get paranoid, and imagine things."

"Well, if you don't have anything definite, what is it that has you worried, then?" I asked.

"For starters, take my band. Not the band I have now. Since I made it big, I took on an agent and promoters and they brought in hotshot, polished Nashville musicians for me to front. I'm talking about the original five boys that barnstormed around with me, playing the border honkytonks on Saturday nights where we ducked flying beer bottles. In the last year, those boys have been getting killed off, one by one. Billy Joe Turner, my drummer, was run over one night last January by a hit-and-run driver who was never caught. Couple of months later, Addie Davis, who played electric bass with me, was found in an alley, beaten to death. The cops said it was a mugger. They're still looking for him. Early this summer, Tommy Mason, steel guitar, burned to death when his mobile home caught on fire. Tommy had been seen at a bar drinking pretty heavy that evening. The fire marshal said he figured Tommy came home and passed out in bed with a lighted cigarette.

"Miss McHaney, those boys were like family back when things were tough, when we played for a few bucks a night and drinks. Now that I'm up in the big-time money, playing Las Vegas dates, featured on the Grand Ole Opry, those boys can't even play with me. I got this hotshot promoter says I got to use slick city musicians out of Nashville who look down their nose at honky-tonk musicians like Tommy Mason, Billy Joe Turner, and Addie Davis. Says they ain't good enough.''

There were tears in his eyes. "I couldn't take my boys into the big-money circuit with me. They died broke. Now only two of them are left: my fiddle player, Crawfish Willie Atkins, and my sax player, Jimmy Joy Jamison. And they're as scared as I am, wondering who's killing us off and who's gonna be next.''

The word he'd used earlier, *paranoid*, rattled around in my mind. Maybe he *had* been smoking funny cigarettes. But if it was some kind of imagined persecution, it was real enough to Freddie Landers. The poor guy was obviously scared spitless. And I had to admit that three accidental deaths in less than a year was a pretty spooky coincidence.

"Has anything happened that makes you think someone is trying to kill you?" I asked.

"There was that food poisoning I got at the chili cookout at my ranch on the Fourth of July. I was sick as a dog. Like to have died. Everybody figured I just got ahold of some spoiled food, but it seems pretty darn peculiar to me that nobody else at the party got sick. Then, just last week, I was setting up some amplifying equipment in the music room in the basement of my home, and I darn near got electrocuted. I got a shock that knocked me out for several minutes. Later, I called in an electrician and he found some bare wires that shouldn't have been there. Says he can't figure out how it happened. Well, I know how it happened. Somebody's killing off everyone in my original band, and now they got a contract out on me." He mopped his brow with a shaking hand.

I stared at him, feeling a chilly sensation run up my spine. "Do you have any idea why anyone would do that?"

Freddie shook his head, looking scared and baffled. "I'm an easygoing guy. I don't go around making enemies. I just play my guitar and write my songs. Still, since I started making all this money, I'm dealing with a whole bunch of people I never knew about before—agents, promoters, groupies. There are the land developers who keep on my back about that country-western theme park we're building. There are the people in the businesses I own in the valley. Now the movie people are down here shooting the movie about my life and career. There's even my wife."

"Your wife?"

"Yeah. I hate to say this, but I married Lorraine a year ago, after we'd known each other just a couple of weeks. She's a beautiful woman, and I'm just crazy about her. But the fact of the matter is, I don't know a whole lot about her. She claimed to come from a wealthy family, the Wingers, who owned property up at Rio Dulce. Said her parents died and left her a lot of money. The way I met her was when she outbid me for an expensive Arabian mare at a horse auction. I fell head over heels, and we flew to Las Vegas and tied the knot. But since then I've wondered if she's told me the truth about her past. She claims she was never married before, but she don't act like a woman who's never been married. And I'm not so sure she's from Rio Dulce the way she claims. Some people from there I've talked to don't seem to know anything about her family. If they were as well-off as she says, it seems they'd be well-known around there. It would just break my heart if Lorraine was mixed up in this somehow. I can't tell you how much I love that woman. But I'm just about at the point that I don't trust anybody. Lorraine would be a rich woman if I died. Besides my property and bank account and royalties from my songs that she'd inherit, there's a joint million-dollar life-insurance policy we took out recently.''

I have to admit that caught my attention.

He handed me a wallet-size color photograph of his wife. Lorraine Landers was, indeed, a striking woman. She was about thirty years old, blond, pretty. Her makeup was skillfully applied. Looking at the picture, I saw class, polish, sophistication. Whatever or whoever Lorraine Landers might be, she was definitely no flashy bimbo or country-western groupie.

"Then," Freddie added, "there's my ex-wife, Tammie Sue. She was the female vocalist in my band when I first got started. She's got a terrible temper, and she can get downright vicious, especially when she's been drinking.

Once when we were married, she threw a beer bottle at me, and another time she ran me out of the house with a butcher knife. I wouldn't put anything past that woman.''

"Would she profit by your death?"

"Maybe not in money, but she'd as soon kill me as look at me. See, Tammie Sue and I was married in the early days when I was so broke we barely had a roof over our heads. I got tired of her drinkin' and her temper and divorced her. Then my songs hit it big and the money started rolling in. Now, Tammie Sue's still back in that ratty old trailer house we lived in, while I'm drivin' around in a Cadillac with a flashy new blond wife. Tammie Sue's fuming and so jealous she can spit venom. Nothing would pleasure her more than to see me dead.''

I could see I was going to have my work cut out for me. Freddie's life appeared to be populated with the makings of a TV series soap-opera cast.

I nibbled at my bottom lip, wondering what I was getting into here. In spite of the seemingly incredible coincidence, the deaths of the three musicians from his first band could have been nothing more than freak accidents. The kinds of lives those honky-tonk musicians lead don't exactly qualify them as good insurance risks. The police had obviously checked out the deaths and found nothing to indicate homicide. Freddie's "food poisoning" episode and the near electrocution could also have been completely accidental.

On the other hand, Freddie was a wealthy man and a celebrity. When you get into the world of big bucks and public figures, all kinds of kinky things are possible.

This was not the kind of case I was used to dealing with. Still, if Freddie was willing to shell out the price of my fee to allay his suspicions, flimsy though they appeared to be, why should I turn down his money? And if I were to discover a hit man (or woman) among his acquaintances, thereby saving Freddie's life, I would more than earn my fee.

A lawyer friend I sometimes did some investigating for had written up a contract for me to have my clients sign. It had enough "whereases" and "to fors" to be impressive. The purpose was to make sure I got paid and to keep me from being sued. Whether it would really do that, I wasn't sure. Fortunately, so far I hadn't needed to find out.

Freddie gave the paper a cursory glance and agreed to the five-hundred-dollar advance without a murmur. I think he was so worried and distracted, he didn't care what he was signing.

"How are you goin' to go about checking this out?" he asked.

That was a good question. Off the top of my head, I wasn't sure myself. So I improvised. "I'll start by asking questions. I'll look over the people you mentioned. I'll see what I can find out about the members of your band who were killed. I may check on your wife's background. She looks like the person who would profit the most if something happened to you."

Perspiration was again beading Freddie's forehead. He patted it with a monogrammed handkerchief. "Just be careful she don't find out," he said uneasily. "It would be awful if Lorraine discovered I hired a private detective to check on her. She'd more 'n likely walk out on me. I sure don't want that to happen if she's innocent."

"I'll be discreet. I ought to have a talk with your ex-wife too. Where would I find her?"

"Tammie Sue? Probably in some bar when she ain't sleeping off a binge in the trailer. It's parked at the Palm

Grove Park in Willow Springs. Some days she's around where the movie company is shooting on location. They're using her in the movie.''

"The movie about your life?'' I asked with surprise. "*The Freddie Landers Story?*''

"It wasn't my idea,'' he grumbled. "The director thought it would be an authentic touch, since we started out together. She sings some numbers. She can still belt out a song when they can catch her sober.''

I made a mental note to put Tammie Sue high on my list of people to meet. I also needed to check on his present wife. "Did you say Lorraine's maiden name was Winger?''

Freddie nodded. Then he said, "You can meet Lorraine tomorrow at the barbecue. It'll give you a chance to meet a lot of the people I've been talking about. The movie people will be there and the land developer who's involved in the Freddie Landers theme park. Some other business associates will be there.''

"Okay. What shall I wear?''

"Blue jeans like you got on now are fine. I don't go in for a lot of highfalutin social stuff. Lorraine likes to give parties where I got to wear a tuxedo. I hate that. Tomorrow is my kind of party. Plenty of barbecued spare ribs and pinto beans and kegs of cold Lone Star Beer and a band of mariachis strummin' guitars.''

I grinned. "That's my kind of party, too, Freddie.''

He smiled for the first time since coming into my office. "I reckon you an' me's gonna get along just fine, Miss McHaney.''

Freddie and I shook hands. His palms felt cold and sweaty. He gave me the kind of desperate look that someone sinking in deep water would give a lifeguard. Then he hurried out.

I couldn't help feeling sorry for the guy. Maybe his fears were imagined, but they were real enough to him. I had the uneasy feeling they might indeed be real.

After he left, I finished up my paperwork, then locked up the office and went down to the parking lot, where my battered pickup had been roasting in the August sun all day.

My office is in Brownsville, a city near the southern tip of the Rio Grande valley, a few miles from the Gulf of Mexico. I can leave the city behind in a few minutes. Then I take a scenic route through some lush, semitropic countryside to the Intercoastal Canal, where I live on a houseboat.

Before the turn of the century all this was barren, desertlike prairie covered with scrubby brush and mesquite, not much good for anything but supporting coyotes and a few scraggly herds of longhorn cattle. Then some developers thought about the warm climate not unlike southern California's and Florida's. They eyed all the water flowing down the nearby Rio Grande and got the bright idea of digging irrigation canals called *resacas*. That transformed the desolate, arid southwest tip of Texas along the Rio Grande and the Gulf coast into a garden spot lush with tropical vegetation. Citrus orchards and truck gardens flourished. The scrubby chaparral had been replaced with stately palm trees, banana and avocado trees, and great clumps of scarlet bougainvillea.

To a person like me, who had grown up in Spanish Harlem in the canyons of Manhattan, this was paradise. When I'd hitchhiked my way out of New York five years ago, I was headed for California. I stopped off in Dallas, forced to sling hash in a diner for a few months to replenish my bankroll.

One night a couple of kids, one with a bad case of acne, the other skinny as a bean pole, both with exaggerated ideas of how tough they were, came into the diner to pull a heist. They wore leather vests and chains. Real macho. Both were armed with knives. I didn't try to stop them when they cleaned out the cash register. When you're from New York, you learn that the smartest thing to do in cases like that is to keep your mouth shut and give them what they want. But then they started roughing up the customers, and when it looked as if the skinny one was going to cut a gray-haired woman who'd gotten up from a booth to protest, something in me snapped. I have a trait that has gotten me into a lot of trouble: a notoriously hot temper, probably the result of a volatile blood mixture—a Latin mother and an Irish father. I yanked off my apron and came around from behind the counter in a boiling rage.

"Hey, you," I said in Spanish. "Leave the lady alone."

"Yeah, and who's gonna make me?" the skinny one said, jerking around to give me a wild look.

I could see he was loaded to the eyeballs with crack. I knew all the signs: the frantic note in his voice, the glassy, wild look in his eyes. I was taking a chance, but at that moment, my sense of justice overrode my common sense.

"You think you're pretty bad, don't you?" I sneered.

"Yeah, I'm bad all right, and you're in big trouble, lady," he said, coming at me with his switchblade.

"Hey, man, you ain't seen bad," I told him. "*Now* you're looking at *real* b-a-a-d."

I remember thinking as he jabbed wildly with his knife

that this clumsy punk wouldn't last three minutes in a street fight where I came from. I'm five-seven and slender, but I'm wiry and tough from the streets where I grew up, and I have a black belt in karate. I caught the punk's wrist. He had a startled look as I spun him into the counter, where he sent saltshakers and ketchup bottles scattering. Before he could straighten up, I gave him a hard chop at the back of his neck. His face slammed down on the counter and the knife clattered out of his hand. I scooped it up and turned to Acne-face. By then I was really mad.

But the kid with the pitted complexion had appraised the situation and was giving the whole matter serious reconsideration, especially when he saw the knife in my hand and the manager on the phone dialing 911. Acne-face scooted out of the place, abandoning his *compadre*, who was sitting on the floor in front of the counter, nursing a broken tooth, looking dazed.

The police picked up the skinny punk. The gray-haired woman who nearly got herself cut came over to thank me. And that was how I got into the private-eye business.

It turned out that the woman, Sarah Wilson, was a licensed private investigator who specialized in tracking missing persons. She was a chunky, middle-aged woman with short-cropped steel-gray hair, but don't let her grandmotherly appearance fool you. Sarah is one of the best in her field. I wound up working for her.

I owe Sarah a lot, not only for giving me a job and the things she taught me, but for taking me under her wing and helping me turn my life around. Mostly, I thank her for just being my friend. Sarah has a great compassion for people who've had a hard time.

I talked a lot to Sarah about what my life had been like before I met her.

I was born in Puerto Rico. My mother was Puerto Rican. My father was an Irish seaman who came ashore while the oil tanker he was sailing on was docked. He was my mother's second husband. He stopped by a few times when his ship was in port, but he lost interest in raising a family and eventually sort of disappeared. I don't remember him at all.

I had my Irish father to thank for my last name, fair complexion, dark red hair, and sprinkling of freckles in a family where I had five half sisters and three half brothers, all as brown as pecans. I did inherit my best feature, large brown eyes, from my mother.

When my mother moved us to New York, my fair complexion got me a lot of taunts and fights. I grew up streetwise and tough on New York's Upper West Side.

Life was cheap where I lived. By the time I was twenty, a lot of my friends and relatives were dead—either OD'd or killed in gang fights. I made the decision that that wasn't going to happen to me. I had ambitions to make something out of my life. I had dropped out of school for a while, but I went back and got my high-school diploma.

One day, shortly after my twentieth birthday, I decided to leave town and start a new life. The next thing I knew I was on the road, sticking my thumb out, headed for California because it was the place that seemed so great in the movies, all warm and green and sunny.

Instead, I wound up in Texas working for Sarah. We went all over the state on her calls to find missing persons. That was how I became acquainted with the Rio Grande valley.

I worked for Sarah for five years. Then I decided to set up my own business.

In Texas, you apply to a state board for a private investigator's license. One requirement is a year's experience in police or investigative work, which I had with Sarah. Another requirement is no felony record. Fortunately, in spite of all the bad things that had happened in my tough neighborhood back home, I'd managed to stay pretty clean.

I picked Brownsville to set up my business. The semitropical valley satisfied my fantasies of southern California. And I found a houseboat for rent cheap on the Intercoastal Canal a short drive from town. It was perfect. On weekends I fished off my back porch and dabbled with oil paint and canvas. I'd taken up painting when Sarah told me it would be good for my nerves. I'd actually sold a few of my paintings to tourists who didn't know any better.

Now, as I neared the coast, the growth of tropical vegetation gave way to the open coastal flats. I drove off the main road and followed a road that skirted the Intercoastal Canal. I drove past bait shops, boat ramps, a diesel repair shed, rows of shrimp boats tied up at the wharves. Then I arrived at my houseboat.

When I parked the pickup, my dog, Bismark, came bounding from the houseboat deck to greet me. Bismark is a fancy name for a big, shaggy black-and-white animal of uncertain ancestry. He's what we call an air-scent dog. He can pick up human scent that is days old. Sarah helped me train him. I had used him successfully on a number of search-and-rescue cases. Now he rolled around at my feet to express his ecstasy at seeing me, then lay on his back, exposing his stomach to show his submission and trust. I knelt to rub his stomach and scratch his ears. I felt secure with Bismark on guard beside my bed at night. He had a bellow that would scare a hit man into the next county. With Bismark trotting happily beside me, I stepped onto the deck of my abode. The cabin is made of weathered, gray boards built atop an old barge hull. It is not a thing of beauty, but it is home and the rent is cheap.

Inside, I have one large main room that contains a bed, a chest of drawers, a table, some comfortable chairs, my stereo, a small portable TV, and some shelves crammed with books. In one corner is an old-fashioned barber's chair. That's right, a barber's chair. I found it in a junkyard. I love it. When I tilt it back at the right angle, it's the most comfortable chair in the world. I spend hours reading in it.

A compact galley unit is housed in an alcove. One door leads to a small bathroom, another to a closet. That's it, pretty bare and essential. But at night, there is a gentle rocking motion that lulls me to sleep, and the breeze is always cool and smells of fish and salt.

I took a quick shower, changed into fresh blue jeans and shirt, and walked down to Catfish Charlie's place, a half mile up the canal.

Catfish Charlie Barton was one of my more colorful neighbors. He was also my landlord. The houseboat where I lived actually belonged to Charlie. He rented it to me for a ridiculously low price because, I suspect, he thought he had unofficially adopted me.

Charlie served the best popcorn shrimp on the waterfront. He was somewhere in his seventies, tough as leather and sunburned to a worn-saddle brown with a contrasting crown of snow-white hair. He had a courtly air about him and a charm that wouldn't quit. Also, he was a very interesting man, though I suspected he never let the truth stand between him and a good story. Charlie had been everywhere and had done everything. According to him, he had fought in Spain in the thirties; had been a newspaper reporter; had met Mussolini, Franco, FDR, Haile Selassie, Hitler, and Howard Hughes; was a bomber pilot in World War II; and had worked as an FBI agent and a CIA spy. If half the things he claimed to have done and been were true, it would make one heck of a book, which he claims to have been writing for the past ten years.

Catfish Charlie's place was a ramshackle building constructed of raw lumber sitting on pilings at the end of a short, private pier. It was just sitting there waiting for the first hurricane to come along and blow it away. Inside, for decorations, Charlie had hung fishnets, life preservers, shark skulls, and driftwood. There was a long bar, tables, and booths, all looking battered. The jukebox was playing a Tommy Dorsey big-band record. Charlie wouldn't allow any rock or country-western records on his machine, a fact which made a lot of customers mad. Charlie didn't give a hoot.

As soon as I walked in and sat at my favorite booth by a window overlooking the water, Charlie brought a platter of fresh-fried popcorn shrimp, hush puppies, and a glass of cold beer.

"Hi, kid. How's my favorite lady PI?" he asked, taking a seat in the booth facing me. Charlie had a voice like a rusty diesel engine in low gear.

"Hungry," I said, diving into the shrimp.

"Here. Use some of this remoulade sauce." He pushed it toward me.

"Hey, Charlie," a thirsty customer called from the bar. Charlie ignored the man.

The shrimp were delicious. I swallowed some of the cold beer.

"How's business?" Charlie asked. He liked to talk shop with me. He was hoping I'd give him the details of a case I was working on so he could offer free advice. I thought I owed my clients professional confidentiality. That irritated Charlie no end. He had a curiosity bump a mile high.

"Charlie," I said, "There's a chance I'm going to be away for several days. Will you feed Bismark for me until I get back?"

"Sure. Working on a case, huh?"

"You might say that."

"Weekend stakeout?"

"Not exactly."

"Well, be careful. Hate to lose a steady customer."

Somehow, I wished he hadn't said that.

Chapter Three

I was up early the next morning. The sun was just above the horizon, spreading a rosy path over the water. I paused for a moment to watch a couple of barges moving in stately procession behind a tug headed north up the Intercoastal Canal. Then I slammed the truck door and turned the key.

I headed out on one of the countless farm-to-market roads that crisscross the valley like spiderwebs. Then I was on US Highway 83. Locally, it has been nicknamed the longest main street in the world because it links a chain of small valley towns—Pharr, Donna, Mercedes, La Feria. When you leave the city limits of one, you immediately enter the next.

I was on my way to Rio Dulce to see what I could find out about Freddie's glamorous current wife. But first I wanted to meet the first Mrs. Landers.

Willow Springs was just a short detour out of my way. I got there about eight-thirty and stopped at a service station to ask directions to the Palm Grove Trailer Park.

21

Like other trailer parks in the valley this time of the year, most of the RV spaces were empty. They would be filled when the winter tourists arrived. Now, a few spaces were occupied by year-round residents in mobile homes. This park would obviously not rate a triple-A in the Woodall travel trailer guide. The concrete slabs in the small lots were cracked and grease stained. The small lots were grown up in grass and weeds around dilapidated mobile homes that had seen better days. A few had rusty metal storage sheds, and several had screened cabanas with sagging roofs.

Just inside the park entrance was a mobile home bearing a sign, *Office*. I parked the truck and walked up to the narrow porch. Inside I could hear kids yelling and a TV blaring. I rang the bell several times before a plump woman with a yelling infant on one hip came to the screen door.

"I'm looking for Tammie Sue Landers's trailer," I said, raising my voice to override the child's howling.

"Number twelve," the woman yelled back.

Back in the truck, I followed a narrow, winding road that meandered between the trailer lots. There were numerous speed bumps designed to jar you into remembering the speed limit was five mph.

Number 12 was a back lot. The trailer home on it looked even more dilapidated than its neighbors. One corner sagged wearily. Beside it on the cracked concrete slab was a rusty, dark-green 1975 Pinto with a cracked windshield and a flat tire. When I stepped out of the truck, I caught a whiff of backed-up sewer line.

The shades in the mobile home were drawn. I pushed a doorbell, decided it wasn't working, and knocked instead. I knocked several times with no response.

A woman in a housecoat and wearing curlers came out

of the trailer next door to pick up her morning paper. "She's home," she called to me, "but she don't get up till past noon." She grinned. "Hung over."

"Thanks," I said. "Maybe I can wake her."

The woman shrugged, her expression telling me I was wasting my time.

I kept at it. Eventually, persistence paid off. I heard noises inside, furniture bumped, muttered curses. The door opened. The face that peered out at me gave me a surprise. Freddie had robbed the cradle the first time around. The drinking, pills, and late hours had taken their toll, but under the wreckage, I saw a woman in her early twenties. Her stringy blond hair was a tangled mess. There were dark smudges under her bloodshot eyes. She was barefooted and wearing only a long T-shirt. The smells of sour beer and stale cigarette smoke drifted through the screen door.

"Tammie Sue?" I asked

"Who th' heck are you?" Her voice was a husky croak.

"My name is Kate McHaney. Can I talk to you for a few minutes?"

She blinked at me, struggling to organize some semblance of order in her befuddled thinking processes. "Do you know what time it is?" she demanded, her voice cracking with indignation.

"A little past eight-thirty. I'm sorry to wake you up, but I was on my way by here and I do need to talk to you."

"What for?"

I'd once had a printer make me up an assortment of business cards with various business and professional titles beside my name. At a moment's notice, I could whip out a card listing me as everything from a CPA to a truant officer. Now I handed Tammie Sue a very official-looking press card bearing my name.

"I'm a writer. I'm putting together a piece about the movie that they're filming about Freddie Landers. I understand you have a part in the movie, and I'd like to interview you."

I rattled that bit of fiction off without blinking an eye.

I waited while her befogged brain cells fumbled with alcohol-clogged circuits. "Yeah, what're you writing this for?"

"Newspapers," I said vaguely. "Maybe a national magazine article."

"Well, come in," she said uncertainly. "Excuse the mess. I haven't had time to clean up today."

That was the understatement of the year. We waded through a sea of old newspapers, empty beer cans, and filled ash trays. She shoved a pile of dirty laundry off a couch, removed a nightgown dangling from a floor lamp, and said, "Have a seat. I'll be right back."

She set an unsteady course for a doorway, then closed the door behind her. I heard water running somewhere in a back room. Behind the door, a man's voice complained. There was an exchange of angry words liberally punctuated with obscenities. Presently, the door opened and Tammie Sue reappeared. She had run a comb through her hair, washed her face, applied some makeup, and put on a robe. "Want some coffee?"

I looked at the kitchen area piled high with unwashed pots, pans, and dishes, over which roaches scurried. "No, thanks," I said.

She shoved some dirty dishes aside and, with hands shaking badly, made herself a cup of instant coffee. She fumbled in a cabinet, located a bottle of Seagram's, and poured a hefty slug of that into the cup. After gulping some of the spiked coffee, she lit a cigarette and took a deep drag. Then she brought the coffee and cigarette over and sat in a chair facing me. "What do you want to know? You're not going to take any pictures, are you? I need to go have my hair styled."

"Nothing like that. Just a little background information for now." I took a notebook and ballpoint pen from my purse and tried to look journalistic. "I understand you sang with Freddie's band when he was first starting. You were married to him then."

"Yeah," she said sullenly. "That louse."

"I gather it wasn't a friendly divorce?"

"Not exactly. I hate his guts. He's nothing but a third-rate honky-tonk musician. If it hadn't been for my singing, he never would have got any bookings when he started out. Now he's turned into a big shot, and he thinks he's too good for the musicians who got him started."

"I heard some of the guys in his first band have died recently."

She turned pale. The cup and saucer rattled in her hand. She took a quick gulp of her Seagram's-laced coffee. "Billy Joe Turner, Addie Davis, and Tommy Mason," she whispered, her voice unsteady.

I stared at her. Her fear was almost palpable in the stale, musty air of the trailer home. "Were you friends with them?"

"Of course. We were in Freddie's band together."

"Do you know anything about their deaths?"

She shook her head. She had drawn her feet up under

her and was huddled in her chair in a fetal position. "Look, I don't want to talk about them."

I was silent for a moment, digesting her reaction. She looked as scared as Freddie when he came to my office yesterday. Was she, too, afraid that all the members of Freddie's band were being stalked by a crazed killer who was picking them off, one by one, and that she might be next on the list?

I changed the subject. "How did Freddie feel about the musicians he played with back when he was starting out?"

"Wouldn't give them the time of day once he hit the big time."

"Were they bitter?"

"That's putting it mildly."

"How about the two musicians from that first band who are still living? How do they feel about Freddie?"

"They hate his guts, same as I do."

"Enough to want to kill him?"

She gave me a strange look. "What kind of a question is that?"

"I'm trying to find out how deep the feelings are running. You're making this movie with Freddie. It's an interesting situation for magazine readers. They'd like to know how you feel, being on the movie set with your ex-husband, singing with his band again."

"It ain't his band," she said bitterly. "His band is those three guys who died and the two that are still living, Crawfish Willie Atkins and Jimmy Joy Jamison and me. We were his real band. What he's got now are a bunch of hot shots out of Nashville who laugh behind his back because he's a no-talent bum."

"But he's written all those hit songs."

"Lucky fluke," she sneered.

"You haven't told me how you feel when you have to do a scene with him in the movie they're filming."

She took another deep lungful of smoke, held it, then let it drift from her nostrils. She polished off the rest of the spiked coffee. Tears filled her eyes again. "All right, I'll tell you how I feel. Tell your readers I'm real sorry it wasn't Freddie who burned up in his bed instead of poor Tommy Mason, or got run over instead of Billy Joe Turner."

When I left, she was back at the kitchen sink, pouring another slug of Seagram's into her cup, leaving out the coffee this time.

As I drove away, I thought that Freddie was partly right. Tammie Sue did hate him and would probably be delighted if he was the next to get killed. I had serious doubts, however, that she could have poisoned his chili or rigged his amplifying equipment to give him a fatal shock. I was more impressed by how frightened she was.

I pulled into Rio Dulce shortly after nine o'clock and found a parking spot on Main Street. The mouth-watering smells of frying bacon and fresh coffee drifting out from a café reminded me that I had not had breakfast. I followed the aromas into the Rose Café and took a seat at the counter. A plump, smiling Mexican-American waitress took my order for *huevos rancheros*, toast, grits, and coffee. Since moving South, I had developed a taste for grits with breakfast.

The small café was bustling with the breakfast rush hour. The air was hazy with cigarette smoke and oily steam from the grill. Amid the clatter of dishes, there was a medley of voices, mostly speaking Spanish. Being this close to the border, these valley towns were predominantly Mexican-

American, although there were floods of the winter tourists from the Midwest every October.

Someone put a coin in the jukebox. Appropriately enough they had picked Freddie Landers singing his hit composition "Remember Our Yesterdays." Real crying-in-your-beer music. I hadn't heard it in a while and now I listened more carefully. I have to admit I like country-western songs, and I could see why this one was such a big seller. The melody had a haunting, original quality that was Freddie's trademark. I had to hand it to the guy. Despite Tammie Sue's jaundiced appraisal, Freddie Landers was a musical genius.

The song reminded me why I was here. While I waited for my breakfast, I went over to a public phone near the cash register and consulted the book. There were no Wingers listed, which was the maiden name Freddie said Lorraine had used. He said she told him her parents were deceased, but I thought there might be some distant relatives in the area.

After breakfast, I asked directions to the local library. There I leafed through old issues of the city directory. I had to go back five years before I found one listing the name Winger—a Mr. and Mrs. Henry Winger and family at 514 Topeka. It gave his occupation as employee of the electric utility company. That didn't sound like the kind of wealthy parents from whom Lorraine claimed she had inherited big bucks, but so far it was the only lead I had turned up. Maybe somebody in the neighborhood would remember the Winger family.

From the librarian, I got directions to Topeka Street. It was a residential area of middle-income, one-story two-and-three-bedroom brick homes. There were the thick groves of banana trees, splashes of red bougainvillea, and sprinklers watering green lawns that were typical of well-kept homes in these valley residences.

I found 514 and started there. The woman who answered the door looked harassed, as if I'd caught her in the middle of housecleaning. No, she said impatiently, she didn't know anything about the people who had owned the house before her. The previous owners had moved out of state and left the property in the hands of a realtor from whom she and her husband bought the place.

I tried the next three houses in a row with no better luck. Then I noticed an elderly man across the street, clipping his hedge. I crossed over and approached him. "Hi."

" 'Mornin', ma'am," he said. He patted his shiny bald head with a handkerchief. "Hot already, isn't it?

"Sure is."

"Bet we hit a hundred by this afternoon."

"Wouldn't be surprised."

We exchanged smiles. I like old people. There's something kind and nonthreatening about them. A lot of them have a wry sense of humor. My guess was that this gentleman was retired and puttering around his yard to pass the morning.

"I'm Kate McHaney," I said, holding out my hand.

"Pleased to make your acquaintance, ma'am. Bill Dickenson is my name."

"Have you lived here long, Bill?" I asked, nodding at his neat, well-kept house.

I could see he was pleased and flattered that a young woman would call him by his first name.

"Twenty-five years. I built this house. Raised my family here."

"Then you know this neighborhood pretty well."

"Sure do."

"I've been trying to get some information about a family who lived at 514. The Wingers. Did you know them?"

"Well, I certainly did. Henry and Margaret Winger. We were very good friends. In fact, Henry and I both worked for the utility company. They sold their place and moved up North when Henry retired. I sure was sorry to see them go."

"Did they by any chance have a daughter named Lorraine?"

The smile faded. "Yes." He sighed. "It was so sad about Lorraine. Beautiful girl. They never got over that terrible loss." He gave me a puzzled look. "Why on earth are you asking about Lorraine Winger after all these years?"

I told him part of the truth. "I'm a private investigator. I have a client who asked me to try to locate the Wingers."

"A lady private detective? Not many of those around, are there?"

"More than you'd suspect."

"Well, we still get Christmas cards from the Wingers. I can get you their address if you want."

"Thanks. That would be helpful. What can you tell me about Lorraine?"

"The poor child was killed by an automobile on Christmas Eve. She was riding her bicycle just a few streets over from here."

"How old was she?"

"Eight, I think. Maybe seven going on eight."

I didn't think I'd have any need of the Wingers' current address, but I got it from Bill Dickenson anyway. Then I drove to the town's cemetery. A caretaker gave me directions to Lorraine Winger's grave site. I stared at the dates on the stone. The Lorraine buried here was born on May 8, 1960. If she were alive today, she would be the same age as Freddie Landers's Lorraine.

The headstone gave me an eerie feeling. Had Lorraine Winger returned from the grave to marry Freddie Landers?

Chapter Four

T hat, of course, was ridiculous. There was a much more rational explanation. Taking a name from a gravestone was a way of establishing a new identity. The woman Freddie was married to could have strolled through this cemetery, looking for a person with a birthdate close to hers. After finding Lorraine Winger's grave, she might have asked around and found the Winger family had moved to another state. Then it would have been a simple matter to request a copy of Lorraine Winger's birth certificate from the county clerk. Armed with that as a basic ID, she could have built up a whole new identity, applying for a driver's license, opening a bank account, getting credit cards, all in the name of Lorraine Winger.

Looks as if your suspicions about her being a phony are right, Freddie, I thought sadly. The poor guy was going to be crushed.

This situation was really beginning to disturb me. When Freddie had told me of his suspicions, I had been skeptical.

Now it was becoming clear that the woman he'd married was an impostor. But who was she? What was she hiding? Where had she come from? What was her game? Was she a potential murderer? She certainly had the motive: a million-dollar life-insurance policy. Wow!

I spent a few more hours in Rio Dulce. First I made the rounds of the motels, showing the desk clerks Lorraine's picture. As strikingly attractive as she was, I thought she might be remembered. There were only three major motels in the town. The desk clerk at the Holiday Inn did, indeed, remember her. "Yeah, she stayed here for several weeks about a year ago. A real classy lady. I remember she drove a flashy red Cadillac and she had real expensive luggage. Always dressed to the teeth." He added, "A guy was in here a couple of weeks ago asking about her."

That took me by complete surprise. For a moment I wondered if my ears were playing tricks. "Are you sure the man was asking about this woman?"

"He had a picture that looked just like this one."

"What did this fellow look like?"

"Oh, sort of average. Kind of sandy hair. Middle-aged. The thing I remember about him was that he had only one arm. Right arm, I think. The other was just an empty sleeve pinned up."

For a moment I was at a loss for words. Somebody else was on the trail of Lorraine's past. Who could it be?

"The woman in this picture—do you remember where she came from?"

He shook his head. "I think her car had out-of-state plates, but I don't remember what state."

I knew I'd have to go through all kinds of company red tape to get them to dig her registration out of files a year old. It might even take a court order. Anyway, I doubted if reading the registration card would tell me much. If she was going to all this trouble to establish a new identity, she surely would have lied on the motel register.

There was one other thing I wanted to find out. Freddie said he met her when she outbid him at an expensive horse auction. She sure couldn't have kept an Arabian horse in her motel room.

I learned that there was a riding stable a few miles from town. I drove out there. The stable owner was a tobacco-chewing gossipy type, the kind investigators love. When I showed the stable owner Lorraine's picture, he said, "Oh, sure. Miss Winger. She stabled her horse with us for a while last year. Beautiful animal. Must have cost her a bundle."

"Did she ride any?"

"Ride? No. I don't think I ever saw her ride. She gave us instructions to exercise the horse. She's married to Freddie Landers, the famous country-western singer, y'know. After they got hitched, she came over with a trailer one day and hauled the horse over to Mr. Landers's place."

The scenario was becoming uncomfortably clear. This attractive, stylish woman had arrived on the scene a year ago from who-knows-where, set up a new identity, then very determinedly went about meeting Freddie Landers, even to the extent of laying out big bucks for a horse she didn't need.

If Freddie was correct in fearing that someone was trying to do him in, Lorraine was the most likely suspect I had turned up so far. She had the motive and the opportunity. She could have spiked his chili with some kind of poison and tinkered with his amplifying electronic equipment in an attempt to electrocute him. But then I ran into a curious enigma. Was Lorraine also responsible for the deaths of his three band members? And if so, why? It was easy to see how she would profit by murdering Freddie. But what could she possibly gain from systematically killing the members of his band?

And now a fresh piece had been added to the jigsaw puzzle. Who was the one-armed man who was also on her trail?

Was there some kind of larger plot at work here that I was missing?

I thought about Freddie's first wife, Tammie Sue. I remembered how frightened she was. It was almost as if she knew for certain that someone was killing off the band members one by one and that she was next on the list. Maybe she knew why. Eventually I would need to have another talk with her.

I then headed back down U.S. 83. When I crossed into the county where Freddie lived, I made a stop at the courthouse. This county was also the residence of his original band members. In these small-town, semirural areas, it was the county sheriff's department that handled homicides.

The courthouse was one of those square old sandstone buildings squatting in the town square.

I parked at the curb, turned on the alarm system in my truck, and locked the door. I'd had a very sophisticated alarm system installed in the truck. It's the kind where any kind of motion or tampering with the vehicle will set off lights flashing, the horn blaring, and a siren howling under the hood. It's not that I was worried about anyone's bothering to steal the battered, rusty old truck. I carried an expensive, high-powered Winchester lever-action 30/30, model 94 rifle in the headache rack across the rear window above the backseat, and that could be tempting.

In the detective stories on TV, the private investigator usually packs a handgun in a shoulder holster and mentions somewhere in the story that he has a permit to carry it. There is no such thing as a permit to carry a concealed handgun in Texas except for law-enforcement officers. Even judges are not legally allowed to pack a handgun, though a lot of them do. In real life, half the people in the state have pistols under the seats of their cars or in their handbags, illegal though it may be. But a private investigator can get his license jerked real fast if he or she is caught with a concealed handgun.

It is, however, quite legal to carry a rifle or shotgun in your vehicle if it is in plain view. Such a weapon is a common sight in racks across the rear windows of pickups. The rifle was given to me by a grateful client. I'm too soft-hearted to be a hunter, but I joined a private rifle range and have gotten pretty good at target shooting. I've won several competition shoots. I certainly hope I never have to use the gun in my line of work, but living alone as I do on the houseboat, it gives me a feeling of security.

In the courthouse, I located the sheriff's office. The name on the frosted glass door read, *Steve Gannon, Sheriff, Huisatche County*. I knew quite a few of the law-enforcement officers in the valley, but I had never met this particular one.

When I entered the office, a deputy behind a desk looked up. I gave him my business card and asked to see the sheriff. He told me to have a seat, disappeared into a back office, and returned to tell me that the sheriff was busy; I'd have to wait. Wading into a stack of paperwork on his desk, the deputy paid me no further attention. The pendulum of an old-fashioned wall clock solemnly ticked off the minutes. A window air conditioner hummed.

Patience is a requirement in my line of work.

Eventually the sheriff appeared in his office doorway. Sheriff Steve Gannon was a man in his early thirties, with thick, wavy brown hair that had premature streaks of gray over the temples. He was handsome in a broad-shouldered, rugged, John Wayne sort of way. He wore a tan shirt and trousers immaculately pressed and a heavy, cartridge-studded gun belt with a big, mean-looking .45 Magnum holstered on his hip. His gray eyes were as sharp and piercing as a hawk's. They matched the rock-firm set of his jaw. I had the fleeting thought that I was awfully glad I wasn't here on criminal charges.

"Ms. McHaney, please come in," he invited with a curt nod.

He escorted me into his office, held out a chair for me, then took his place behind his desk. He pinned me with those ruthless hawk eyes.

I shifted uncomfortably, trying to reassure myself that he couldn't possibly know about the time my half brother and I swiped the hub caps on West End Avenue in New York.

He asked, "What can I do for you?"

"As you saw on my business card, I am a private investigator. A man named Freddie Landers hired me yesterday to check into a serious matter. He's afraid that his life is in danger."

Gannon looked exasperated. "I know all about Freddie Landers. He's been in the office several times pestering my deputies, claiming somebody's out to get him. When we try to pin him down, he just gives us vague suspicions.

Nobody has made any threats. He's given us nothing specific. Frankly, I think he's suffering from an overactive imagination.''

"But two attempts have been made on his life," I said heatedly.

"The poisoned chili and the short circuit in his wiring? We checked that out. There's nothing to it. If there's any wiring short circuit, it's in his head."

The fuse on my notoriously short temper was beginning to smolder dangerously. "How can you be so callous?" I demanded. "You're a law officer. You're supposed to protect the lives of the people around here!"

His jaw tightened and his hawk's eyes flared. "Don't you tell me what my duties are, lady."

The last tenuous grasp on my temper snapped.

"Maybe somebody ought to tell you!" I exclaimed, jumping to my feet.

He slowly uncoiled his six-foot frame. His tan had become an angry dull red. "You are about to get yourself in real trouble, Ms. McHaney," he said. "I am very busy. Are you here to file some kind of complaint?"

"Not officially. Not at this time."

"Ms. McHaney, if this is not a police matter and you're not here to file an official complaint, I can't take up the county's time."

"Sheriff Gannon, I came here as an honest tax-paying citizen expecting a bit of courtesy from a public servant. Sorry to have taken your precious time!"

I grabbed my purse and started for the door, but Gannon's voice stopped me. "All right. Cool off. Let's try this again."

I swung around, glaring at him. There appeared to be a

twitch tugging at the corners of his stern mouth. If it was a patronizing smile, I was going to hit him with something if I had to spend the night in the holding cell.

He said in an amused tone, "That's quite a temper you have. It could get you in trouble."

I thought, *It's about to get me in trouble right now, buster.*

He was gazing at me as if really bothering to look at me closely for the first time. There was an element of male appreciation for what he saw that flustered away some of my anger.

In a more conciliatory tone the sheriff said, "Please sit down. I apologize if I have offended you. It's just that private investigators give me a pain in the neck."

"Why is that?" I asked in a tone out of the deep freeze.

"I've had unfortunate experiences with some of your colleagues getting in our way and obstructing police procedure."

He didn't elaborate, and I didn't pursue the matter. It was enough to see that I was dealing with a stubborn man, prejudiced against private investigators, from whom, I could see, I was not going to get much help. To make matters worse, he was probably a male chauvinist to boot.

Nevertheless, I launched into my reason for coming here. "Three local musicians have died in recent months: Billy Joe Turner, Addie Davis, and Tommy Mason. All three of those men played in Freddie Landers's country-western band at one time."

"Yes, I'm aware of that."

"Freddie thinks that someone is killing off his former band members one by one and that he may be next on the hit list. I can see where a number of people would profit by Freddie's death. He's a wealthy man. But I can't see the motive for doing away with his band. They were obscure musicians with no money. The reason I came here was to ask you if you have reason to believe there is some connection between their deaths and what Freddie is convinced are attempts on his life.''

Gannon was silent for a moment, then said, ''Addie Davis was apparently attacked by a mugger in an alley behind the Gypsy Rose, a beer joint where he was playing. The motive was theft. His watch and wallet were taken. We haven't found a suspect. The case is still open. The hit-and-run case, Billy Joe Turner, is also still open, but so far we haven't had any leads on who the driver was. As for the third one, Tommy Mason, the fire marshal ruled out arson. Mason had been drinking heavily that night, and it's assumed he passed out in bed with a lighted cigarette. In answer to your question, no, we don't have any evidence or reason to believe there's any connection between the three deaths.''

''Doesn't it strike you as an incredible coincidence that all three would die within a few months of one another?''

''Life is full of strange coincidences. So far we haven't uncovered anything that would indicate any kind of conspiracy.''

''You don't think there could be some connection between their deaths and Freddie's claim he was nearly poisoned and electrocuted?'' I persisted.

With a note of exasperation, the sheriff replied, ''We went out and looked at the wiring on Freddie's amplifiers. Have you ever seen the electronic equipment these rock musicians use, Ms. McHaney? His music room is the craziest conglomeration of keyboards, electric guitars, basses, control panels, drum machines, speakers, and computers you have ever seen. There are wires everywhere. It's like a jungle of spaghetti. I'm surprised he wasn't electrocuted a long time ago.''

''But after he got knocked flat by a short, he called in an electrician who said the insulation had been stripped from some wires. . . .''

''I spoke with the electrician. I agree there were some bare wires. That doesn't necessarily mean somebody tampered with them. The electrician said the insulation could have been burned off when the short occurred. The point is, we just don't have enough evidence to go around arresting people.''

He leaned forward. ''Ms. McHaney, you look like an intelligent woman. Surely you know that rock musicians are emotional, imaginative people. A lot of them are heavy drug users. They sometimes hallucinate and become paranoid.''

''Yes,'' I said coldly, ''Freddie told me you thought he was just having a bad case of nerves.''

I wondered if I should tell him what I had found out about Lorraine. I decided against that until I had more facts about her. I could see Sheriff Gannon was a practical man who operated only on hard, cold facts.

I left his office feeling it had all been a waste of time. The only thing I had accomplished was to establish that I could expect very little help from the sheriff's department, and that I'd better have plenty of hard evidence if I expected any action from them.

As for the sheriff himself, I found Steve Gannon to be a disturbing man. He was stubborn and infuriating. At the same time, in spite of how angry he'd made me, I was uncomfortably aware of electric sparks flying between us.

The look in his eyes had told me he, too, was very much aware of some kind of potent chemistry boiling between us. It was an unsettling thought that I tried, without much success, to put out of my mind.

Chapter Five

In my truck, I carry a compact Radio Shack lap computer about the size of a loose-leaf notebook. On it, I typed a brief report of my activities in the case to date. When I got back to my office, I'd plug the computer into my printer for a hard copy.

I'm a hi-tech-gadget freak. In my office I have a desktop PC and a fax machine. Now I'm shopping for a cellular telephone for my truck. Sarah convinced me of the importance of electronic equipment in our profession.

Then I was on my way to Freddie Landers's home. It was a sizzling ninety-seven degrees, and the air conditioner in my pickup chose that time to conk out. I had to settle for the hot wind blowing through an open window. I was thankful that at least Freddie had specified casual dress. I had some extra T-shirts and blue jeans in the storage space behind the seat.

Just before I reached the Landers place, I pulled into a rest stop that had comfort facilities. In the rest room, I washed myself off, dried with a paper towel, and slipped into a fresh T-shirt and blue jeans. I ran a comb through my short hair and touched up my scanty makeup. No amount of makeup is going to make me look glamorous. Fortunately, I inherited long, dark eyelashes and sweeping eyebrows from my mother, so my brown eyes look good without mascara and eyeliner. I keep my hair short with bangs that I snip off just above my eyebrows. If I have any vanity, it's over the contrast of my large brown eyes and long eyelashes with my fair complexion. I have been told that brown eyes and red hair are an attractive combination. That, I think, is the best feature in an otherwise ordinary face with freckles and a pug nose.

Feeling refreshed and halfway presentable, I drove the last couple of miles to the Freddie Landers estate. It was a ranch, surrounded by a tall security fence topped with barbed wire. The road crossed a cattle guard and entered between two large concrete pillars that supported a decorative span. Naturally there was a huge wrought-iron guitar in the center of the span.

Inside the grounds, I was stopped by a guard toting a double-barreled shotgun. I could see that Freddie, like a lot of celebrities these days, took the matter of security seriously. I told the guard who I was. He gave me a close look, checked his guest list, asked to see my driver's license, then scowled at the rifle in the headache rack across the back window of my pickup.

"You can't take no guns in here," he said shortly. "You have to check that there rifle with me. You can pick it up when you leave."

I wasn't too happy about parting with the gun, but I didn't think Freddie Landers would steal anything from a guest, and it was reasonable that, as frightened as he was, he wouldn't want someone pulling up to his front door armed with a rifle.

The guard gave me a receipt for the gun. "Nice piece," he said approvingly when I handed it to him.

"Take good care of it," I muttered. Then I headed up the private road that wound between an avenue of palm trees up to the main house, which looked like a set for the TV show *Dallas*.

I was met at the front door by a male servant who directed me through the cool, tile-floored mansion to the patio and pool area at the rear.

The patio looked as if it had been transported from a tropical jungle. I recognized some of the plants, but there were huge ferns and broad-leafed trees that were too exotic for me to identify. Some of the banana trees had full stalks of bananas, and the papayas were laden with green fruit. The area had been landscaped, with clear-water streams cascading down waterfalls and swirling along gravel-bedded streams to quiet pools where sunlight glinted off the shiny scales of giant goldfish. In some of the trees were bright-colored red, green, and yellow parrots, squawking and fluttering among the branches.

There was, of course, a tennis court and the much-publicized swimming pool shaped like a huge guitar. Beyond that were the garages where Freddie kept his imported sports cars and, in the distance, stables and corrals for his fine horses. I could also see a private landing strip and airplane hangar. Freddie Landers definitely went first-class.

The delicious aroma of barbecued beef smoking over smoldering mesquite coals wafted through the air.

I caught sight of Freddie in the midst of the hordes of

guests swarming near an outdoor bar beside the pool. I crossed a low bridge over one of the streams to join them.

Freddie was holding a margarita and from the flush on his cheeks and glazed expression in his eyes, it was not the first of the day. "Folks," he announced loudly, "this here's my little cousin, Miss Kate McHaney, visiting from Laredo. Kate, I want you to meet my friends."

Everyone was there. The crowd included the camera crew shooting his movie. The five top-flight rock musicians from Nashville who made up Freddie's new, slick band were present. Business acquaintances were there. Neighbors had been invited. Relatives had dropped in. Notably missing, however, were the two surviving members of his original band, Crawfish Willie Atkins and Jimmy Joy Jamison, and Freddie's first wife, Tammie Sue, a fact which didn't surprise me.

Freddie guided me through the crowd. First I met Max Brice, an intense man of about thirty, incredibly good-looking, with jet-black eyes and tousled dark hair. Brice was directing the movie about Freddie's life and music. He was something of an anomaly in this gathering. Brice had been the young Hollywood wonder who directed the enormously successful smash hit *Rainbow Gathering*. The film had broken box office records, collected a number of Oscars, and made Brice the hottest young director in Hollywood. He had followed *Rainbow Gathering* with *Tomorrow's End*, a costly extravaganza that flopped dismally, and after that had directed an even worse bomb. After that, the career of Max Brice had nose-dived. He was probably lucky to have landed a job directing this film, which was being produced by a small regional company out of Dallas.

Brice was gracious and friendly when we were introduced. If he was bitter at the downturn in his career, he kept it well hidden.

The next guest I met was Sam Tompkins, the land developer who was putting together Freddie's country-western theme park. Tompkins was a large, bald, cigar-chomping man with a robust voice who looked as if he had been typecast as a used-car salesman rather than a real-estate developer.

Then we moved on to a neat, well-dressed little man in his early forties, whose few remaining strands of hair were arranged to cover as much scalp as possible. Freddie said, "Now, Kate, this here's my cousin, Milton Bowman, the man I owe it all to. Cousin Milton owns the local recording studio that cut my first record, 'Remember Our Yesterdays.' Milton nagged the local DJs into giving the song airtime and . . . well, you know the rest. Milt, shake hands with my little cousin Kate from Laredo.''

Milton Bowman smiled ruefully as he shook my hand. '' 'Course, Freddie's too big for my little studio now, Kate. Those big Nashville recording studios got him all sewed up. Guess I shoulda nailed him with a ten-year contract when I had the chance!''

Did I detect a slight edge under the surface of their good-ole-boy friendly banter?

With his two-tone brown-and-white shoes and striped bow tie, he was a bit overdressed for the party. He wore a chunky diamond on his left pinky. Apparently the recording-studio business was profitable even if he had missed out on an exclusive contract on his famous cousin.

Milton's sharp eyes were looking at me closely as we shook hands. "Kate McHaney," he repeated. "I thought I knew all our relatives. Don't seem to place you. What branch of the family are you from?''

"Second cousins, really,'' I stammered. ''By marriage. Very distant. . . .''

I could see he didn't believe me for a minute. I had the feeling not much got past Cousin Milton.

His wife joined us. She was a plump woman with Cupid's-bow lips. Her plump fingers were sparkling with jewels. ''Elaine,'' Milton said, ''Freddie tells me this young lady is a distant cousin of ours from Laredo. Miss Kate McHaney.''

"McHaney?'' Elaine said, looking at me curiously. ''I don't recollect anyone in the family by that name.''

Freddie broke in, rescuing me from an uncomfortable situation. ''Hey, there's Lorraine! C'mon, Kate, I sure want you to meet my beautiful wife.'' The pride in his voice was heartbreaking in view of what I had found out about her.

The current Mrs. Landers was standing at the elaborate outdoor bar, which was constructed of bamboo and teak wood, giving instructions to the bartender. She turned as we approached, giving me the full impact of her striking appearance. Every strand of her golden hair, exquisitely styled, was in place. Her makeup was skillfully applied. She had classic features: wide-spaced violet eyes; high cheekbones; a slender, delicate nose; and a generous, sensuous mouth. Her trim figure was flattered with lounging pajamas made of a satiny clinging material that probably came from Neiman Marcus and cost more than my houseboat.

Seeing her up close in person, I realized that the photograph Freddie had given me of her had been somewhat misleading. The photographer had softened a tiny tracing of lines around her eyes and mouth. Although she wasn't afraid to show off her figure in the clinging hostess pajamas, her curves gave just a hint of approaching maturity, upon which I suspected she waged unrelenting war at expensive spas.

From the photograph, I had placed her age around thirty. Now I revised that upward by a few years that were hidden by skillful makeup. I also detected an element of calculating hardness in her eyes that had not shown up in the picture.

When Freddie introduced us, Lorraine shook my hand warmly, her voice overflowing with happiness that Freddie had invited me, while her eyes gave me a cool, speculative appraisal. *She doesn't believe for one minute I'm Freddie's cousin, any more than Milton does*, I thought. *Why did I let him talk me into such a dumb masquerade?*

"What can we offer you to drink, Kate darling?" she wanted to know. "Manuel, here, is the best bartender in the valley. I can heartily recommend his margaritas. They're very refreshing on such a hot afternoon."

I would have preferred a beer, but I wasn't going to sound that gauche. "Yes, I'd like a margarita very much."

After that, I circulated among the guests, chatting with them, forming my opinions, trying to decide if any of them was a murderer who was systematically picking off Freddie's musician friends and had him lined up for the next hit. They all seemed innocuous enough, but then murderers do not necessarily have beady, shifty eyes, low brows, and tattoos reading *Born to Kill*.

I did detect undercurrents of bitterness and hostility in Freddie's associates. Oddly, none of it appeared to be directed toward Freddie. Everyone present seemed genuinely

fond of him. It was Lorraine who was the object of sim-
mering resentment.

I got a strong dose of it from Sam Tompkins, the over-
weight realtor, who'd downed several more of Manuel's
potent margaritas by the time I got around to him. His bald
dome was shiny with perspiration and his tongue was giving
him some trouble. He was sitting beside the pool in a deck
chair. He'd changed into swimming trunks, which were
almost lost under his sagging abdomen. Apparently all the
hair that had missed his scalp had sprouted on his chest and
midsection, where it formed a dark, matted forest over the
undulating bulges.

"Enjoyin' th' party, Kate?" he asked thickly.

"Yep."

"Goin' for a swim?"

"No. I didn't bring my swimsuit."

"Too bad," he mumbled regretfully, looking me over in
a way that indicated his disappointment at not viewing me
in a bikini. "I'm goin' in for a dip in a minute."

I thought the pool level was going to rise considerably
when he did.

His bloodshot gaze stretched across the pool to where
Lorraine was chatting with a clump of guests. He looked
at her sullenly. "I notice you met our lovely hostess." His
voice dripped sarcasm and venom.

"Yes. You sound as if you don't you like her."

"Lorraine?" His laugh was a bitter snort. "The woman
is a barracuda." He scowled at me. "Don't tell Freddie I
said that. The poor guy is nuts about her."

"I won't," I promised. "What is it you don't like about
her?"

He took a large gulp of his drink, draining the glass.

"Everythin' changed after Freddie married her. She's takin' over everything. First thing she did was fire Kenneth Mayfield, Freddie's business manager. Really a nice guy, Ken. Was with Freddie for years. Th' man has a wife and kids. Didn't mean a thing to Lorraine. She took over running all of Freddie's business. Got the poor guy hypnotized. We had a nice thing goin' with the theme park before she came along. Now she's takin' that over, changing everything, cutting me out of a lot of the property deals."

Somehow he succeeded in heaving his mountain of flesh out of the deck chair. "Need 'nother drink," he mumbled and went staggering off toward the bar.

His opinion of Lorraine, inflamed though it might have been with alcohol, did not surprise me. She had given me the impression of being a shrewd, calculating businesswoman.

Which brought me to the unpleasant task of making my report to Freddie. I had been putting it off until I could catch a moment to speak to him in private. Also, I thought it kinder to wait until he had a few more drinks under his belt to cushion the blow.

The time came when he wandered over to check on the barbecue and then headed toward the house. I caught up with him just before he reached the patio doorway.

"Freddie, I have to have a word with you."

He gave me a half-apprehensive look. I think he guessed I was going to report what I had learned about Lorraine, and he was afraid of what it might be.

I glanced around to be sure we were alone. Then I told him, "I made a trip to Rio Dulce early today. I checked on Lorraine as you asked me to do. I don't know who she is, Freddie, but she is not Lorraine Winger and she is not from Rio Dulce.''

I thought for a moment that the poor guy was going to cry. "I didn't think she was," he said in a choked voice. Then he asked me plaintively, "Why did she tell me all those lies, Kate?''

"I don't know.''

Briefly I related my other activities, my meetings with his first wife, Tammie Sue, and with Sheriff Gannon. "I don't think Tammie Sue is out to get you, Freddie. I got the impression that she's as scared as you are. I think she has the same notion, that somebody is picking off the members of your band, and she could be next. Are you sure you're telling me everything?''

He nodded, looking miserable. At the moment, I think his fright had been temporarily overcome by his turmoil over Lorraine's lies.

I thought about the one-armed man mentioned by the desk clerk at the Holiday Inn in Rio Dulce. "Freddie," I asked, "do you know any one-armed men?''

He gave me a blank look and shook his head.

Then I said, "I need to know what you want me to do now. All you hired me to do was check out what Lorraine said about her background connections in Rio Dulce. I've done that in less than a day. I haven't figured my expenses, but I'm sure at this point I owe you a refund. The question is, do you want me to dig deeper in this? Do you want me to find out who Lorraine really is, where she comes from? That could be a lot more complicated and expensive. She's apparently from out of state, so it could even involve my taking a flight somewhere.''

"I've got to know," Freddie said distractedly. "Do whatever you have to do to find out the truth. I don't care what it costs."

I touched his arm sympathetically. "It may not be anything serious at all, Freddie. Maybe she just had an unhappy marriage or love affair and wanted to leave it all behind and start a new life. It could be that simple."

He gave me a bewildered look, then turned and walked blindly into the house. He was in a state of shock.

On the surface, the party progressed smoothly. Lorraine announced that the barbecue was ready. The guests lined up. My plate was heaped with succulent barbecued spare ribs and sausage, pinto beans, salad, and chunks of home-made bread. It was delicious. The mariachis, decked out in elaborate Mexican costumes ornately stitched with gold braid, strummed guitars and sang traditional Mexican ballads as they strolled among the guests. It grew darker. The guests grew drunker. There was loud splashing in the pool. The mariachis broke out trumpets.

During a peak in the confusion, I slipped into the house. It seemed deserted. All the activity was outside.

I prowled through the mansion, beginning with Freddie's music room in the basement. Sheriff Gannon's description of the conglomeration of instruments and wires was correct. The items that caught my eye were one gold and two platinum records framed on the wall. Those hit records and his concert tours must have earned Freddie a pile of money.

I then wandered from room to room. The floors were all done in shiny Mexican tile. There was an Aztec motif— white adobe walls; Navajo blankets; great, rugged, open dark beams; enormous fireplaces; bear-skin rugs. There were original paintings, sculptures, and carvings worth a small fortune.

On the second level were the bedrooms. I opened doors until I found the room that I felt must be Lorraine's boudoir. I moved inside and surveyed the room. It was all done in pink and white. Even the original Renoir on the east wall had been chosen to match the color scheme. My vision took in an ornate, antique canopied bed, a dressing table, a chest of drawers, and an antique desk with spindly legs that looked like an authentic Louie something or other. The curtains were pink and ruffled to match the canopy. There was a heavy, scented fragrance in the air, a mixture of powders, colognes, and perfumes emanating from the dressing table. I was ankle-deep in plush white carpet. It was all very feminine and very expensive.

I waded across the carpet and opened a closet large enough to accommodate my houseboat. It was filled with rows of designer gowns suitable for every possible occasion and shelves containing at least a hundred pairs of shoes.

Stepping back out into the bedroom, I saw that a window gave a view of the pool, the tennis courts, the riding stables, and the landing strip. A random thought crossed my mind. I knew that a rock star with the number of hits Freddie had could amass a pile of money. But did he earn this much? Did Lorraine have them living beyond their means on the expectation of cashing in Freddie's million-dollar life-insurance policy? I have a suspicious nature, especially when I see people spending more money than they have.

I looked around the room again. What I hoped to find was some clue to Lorraine's true identity—an old credit card, address book, letters, driver's license. An overload of adrenaline kicked in, speeding up my heart. I have to admit that moments like this, snooping through someone's private belongings in a place where I could get caught any

minute, give me something of a high. They're also scary.
My palms were sweating.

I read once that people often choose professions to satisfy
dark, hidden desires. For example, if surgeons didn't sub-
limate their primitive instincts into acceptable medical roles,
they might be whacking up victims with chain saws. If that's
true, private detectives must be closet voyeurs. Or maybe
we like the thrill of seeing how close we can come to getting
caught.

Whatever the psychodynamics, I had some serious snooping to do, and the question was where to start. The desk
appeared to be the most likely place. I went through it drawer
by drawer, being thorough but careful not to disarrange
things to tip off Lorraine. I found nothing beyond the usual
social notes and credit-card statements. Her checkbook
showed a balance of several thousand, a fact which wasn't
surprising, but there were no unusually large deposits or
withdrawals.

The dressing table yielded nothing except a large assortment of cosmetics. I went though all the drawers in the
chests but found only blouses, underwear, and accessories.

Frustrated, I returned to the center of the room. There
was no other place left to look.

Then I thought about the huge closet. I opened that door,
looking hopelessly at the dozens of handbags. It would take
hours to go through them. There was some expensive luggage on a top shelf. I was able to reach it with the aid of
a convenient ladder. But I could have saved myself the
trouble. It was the kind of luggage that locks with a combination. If I'd had all day, I might have been able to figure
out the combination.

Then something tucked away in the corner of a bottom

shelf caught my eye. It was something totally out of place, a nondescript handbag made of cheap plastic material. What was it doing in this rarefied atmosphere of chic high fashion? Had a maid accidentally left it here?

I opened the bag. Inside was a small bundle of letters postmarked several years ago, addressed to a Madeline Smith. They were mailed from a small town in North Carolina to a Nashville, Tennessee, address. I opened one and quickly scanned the handwriting. It appeared to have been written by a woman named Donna, a friend of Madeline Smith. It contained some hometown gossip, and an allusion to the sad loss Madeline had suffered (apparently a close relative) before leaving her hometown, and prayers and good wishes for Madeline's success in her new job. The letter was dated three years ago.

I replaced the letter and riffled through the other contents of the bag. Mostly it was the usual accumulation one finds in old purses: matchbook covers, outdated aspirin tin, dried-up eyeliner, a few coins, a broken ballpoint pen, a cheap compact. Then there was one item that made me whisper, "Bingo!"

It was a Tennessee driver's license made out to Madeline Smith. The woman in the picture on the license had dark hair, but there was no doubt about who she was. The only difference was that her hair was blond now. She was Freddie Landers's wife, Lorraine.

I quickly scribbled the address on the driver's license and the return address of the letters in a notebook I carry in my jeans pocket.

Feeling quite satisfied with myself, I replaced the purse, closed the closet door, and strode quickly to the bedroom door. As I reached for the knob, it turned. I gasped and took a hasty step backward. The door swung inward. Lorraine stood on the threshold.

We stared at each other.

Chapter Six

I made a quick recovery and went into the best act I could muster under the circumstances. " 'Scuze me," I mumbled in a drunken slur. "Lookin' for th' bathroom." I swayed, grinning apologetically. "Too many margaritas."

Lorraine's reaction was one of narrow-eyed skepticism, debating whether to believe me.

I decided to help her make up her mind. I put my hands over my mouth, widening my eyes. "Oops . . . gonna be sick—"

Lorraine took a horrified look at me standing on her hundred-dollar-a-yard carpet, grabbed my arm roughly, hustled me down the hall to the nearest bathroom, shoved me inside, and slammed the door.

I really wasn't sure if I had convinced her. I made some gagging sounds and flushed the toilet several times in case she was listening outside the door. After an appropriate time, I went back out into the hallway. It was deserted.

Downstairs, the party at the poolside was still in full

swing. I located Freddie. The poor guy had a haggard, haunted look as if his world were crumbling down around him. He was so drunk he could barely stand up. I wasn't sure I could make him understand what I had to tell him. I explained that I'd found a clue to Lorraine's past and that I'd need to fly to Nashville to check it out. He looked at me blankly. I guess my words finally sank in because he mumbled something about leaving early in the morning with the camera crew and being at a border town for the next couple of days shooting some scenes for the movie. I could find him there when I got back.

"Are you feeling better?"

The voice from behind startled me. I turned to face Lorraine. "Yes," I stammered. "I'm terribly embarrassed. I don't usually drink that much."

She shrugged, a cold, thoughtful smile playing around her lips. "Don't apologize. It happens to all of us. Better have some strong coffee before you drive home, though. Ask Manuel for a cup."

"Yes, thanks. That's a good idea."

I hung around a bit longer, but couldn't see that I could accomplish anything else here. I would have liked to have pumped Sam Tompkins some more. The fat real-estate developer was a good source of gossip about the inside track of Lorraine and Freddie's business dealings. But I could see that by now he was totally hors de combat from all the liquor he'd consumed.

I stopped off at the bar where Manuel, the bartender, served me a cup of coffee strong enough to clear up any fuzziness from the margaritas. I made my perfunctory thanks to the host and hostess and said good night to those guests who were sober enough to understand what I was saying.

Then I followed the private road to the gate, where the guard returned my rifle. I was on the main road before the sleepiness hit me. I rolled the window down, letting the cool night air blow in my face. It didn't help. *Darn*, I thought, *that coffee should have perked me up.* I had more than an hour's drive home.

Then strange things began to happen. The road became indistinct. My eyelids became heavy. I blinked my eyes hard. A pair of headlights came straight at me, blinding me. I swerved, trying to avoid them. My reflexes were all haywire. Had I drunk more margaritas than I'd thought? I drove more slowly.

Then the headlights turned and came up behind me, glaring in my rearview mirror. *Why doesn't the idiot pass?* I thought. *He has plenty of room.*

The crash jerked my head back. I cried out. The insane fool had rammed me!

Then he went around me in a tire-screeching spurt, sideswiping me, shoving me dangerously close to a deep ditch on my right. I saw it was a Bronco with big tires. The driver went up the road a piece, turned, and started back at me again.

Now I was both furious and scared silly. Somebody was out here to kill me on this deserted farm-to-market road. I jerked my truck to a stop on the shoulder. I grabbed the Winchester 30/30 from the rack behind me. I worked the lever, hung the gun out the window, aimed several feet above the approaching car, braced the stock against my shoulder, and pulled the trigger. There was only a click as the hammer fell on an empty chamber.

"Oh, no!" I sobbed with mingled fright and fury. The guard back at the gate had unloaded the rifle.

I threw myself down on the seat, bracing myself for the crash as the approaching headlights became blinding spotlights. Again there was a metallic clatter. My truck shook all over from another sideswipe. Frantically, I scrambled in the glove compartment where I kept a box of cartridges. In the dark, I loaded the rifle. This time when I worked the lever, I knew it jacked a live bullet into the chamber.

I stepped out of the truck. My legs had the consistency of rubber. I braced myself against the truck. Down the road, my attacker was turning for another run at me. This time I did not politely aim in the air above the approaching vehicle. I aimed straight for a headlight.

The rifle cracked and bucked in my arm. One of the blinding lights winked out with a clatter of glass. The Bronco came to a screeching halt, slithering all over the road. I jacked another shell into the chamber and fired again, this time aiming just above the roof.

But the driver didn't know that. The Bronco's tires burned rubber as the driver spun around and broke all kinds of speed records getting out of there.

I sank down beside the truck, weak as a kitten, dripping cold perspiration, my teeth chattering. I took several deep breaths before I found the strength to crawl back into the truck.

I started again, keeping one eye on the rearview mirror, but I saw no one following me.

Not that I was all that much better off. My head was spinning wildly. I couldn't focus my eyes. I was weaving all over the road. My arms and legs felt as if they weighed tons. I didn't have the strength to lift my leg from the accelerator to the brake pedal. I heard rushing, hammering sounds in my ears.

A cold, numbing fear began creeping through me, chilling me to the bone. Something was seriously wrong with me. I felt as if I were in the grip of a spine-chilling nightmare.

Then I saw headlights coming up behind me. "Oh, not again," I whimpered.

I drove faster, weaving from one side of the road to the other, struggling to keep my eyelids open. More than anything, I wanted to put my head against the steering wheel and go to sleep. Only bone-chilling fear kept me from giving in to the overpowering drowsiness.

Then I saw a wonderful sight, a revolving, flashing red light above the vehicle behind me. It was the first time in my life I was deliriously happy to be pulled over by a cop.

Ahead of me, the road seemed to split in two. I was approaching a low bridge, but there were two bridges. I was seeing double. I picked the one on the right and came to a rolling stop on the shoulder a few feet before plunging into the water. Then I rested my head against the steering wheel, closed my eyes, and sank into smothering blackness, going down . . . down. . . .

The last conscious thought I had was, *The coffee . . . they put something in the coffee.*

I awoke with a headache that would have put those Excedrin commercials to shame.

Gradually, and with great pain, I became aware of my surroundings. First, I sensed that I was lying on a surface with a thin, uncomfortable mattress. Then, as my eyes focused, I saw a concrete ceiling. I saw bars. I turned over with a groan and looked down at a concrete floor.

I realized another person was in the room. He was seated a few feet away, facing me. I got my vision in better focus.

It was Sheriff Steve Gannon. He was balancing a cup of coffee on a knee, and he was scowling at me darkly.

"Drink this," he commanded, holding out the coffee.

I struggled to a sitting position with another painful groan. I took a sip of the steaming coffee.

"Take this," he ordered. He shook two aspirin from a bottle into my hand.

I swallowed the pills and downed some more coffee. Things came into somewhat sharper focus.

"What am I doing here?" I finally mumbled.

"You were brought in on a DWI charge," the sheriff told me severely.

"Wait a minute! I was not drunk," I said indignantly.

"We found that out when we gave you a Breathalyzer test. What I want to know is what *were* you on? You were weaving all over the highway and then you drove into a ditch. When the deputy brought you in, you were totally incoherent. I want to be accurate when I fill out the report that's going to get your private-investigator license revoked."

I gave him a murderous look. "Suppose I told you I wasn't doing any drugs, that somebody put a Mickey, probably chloral hydrate, in a drink I had at Freddie Landers's party, hoping I'd wreck up my truck and break my neck on the way home."

"Suppose I told you I don't believe you."

"Suppose I demand urine and blood tests right now that'll prove I wasn't using drugs."

Gannon gave me a long, thoughtful look. "Why would somebody at the Landers party want to harm you?"

"Because they thought I was snooping around and might

find out why Freddie's life is being threatened. But that's all just a fairy tale to you, isn't it, Sheriff Gannon?''

Again I saw that faint tug at the corners of his stern mouth. ''Does that temper go along with the Irish name and red hair?''

''From both sides of the family. My mother was Latin. But don't change the subject.''

''You say you were at a party at Freddie Landers's home last night?''

''Yes.''

''Did Freddie invite you?''

''Yes. He wanted me to meet business friends and relatives to see if I could figure out who might want to kill him.''

''Did you find out anything?''

I hesitated. I was not ready to tell him what I'd discovered about Freddie's wife. So she had changed her identity. It still didn't prove she had anything to do with the attempts on Freddie's life or the deaths of his musician friends. I needed to check on her background in Nashville before I had the kind of hard evidence that meant anything to Sheriff Steve Gannon. I thought it was just as well at this point not to mention the Bronco that tried to run me down either. I didn't know for certain it was someone from Freddie's party. It could have been kids high on something out looking for kicks.

''No,'' I said. ''I didn't find out anything.''

''Then why would someone spike your drink with knock-out drops?''

''Maybe I was making someone nervous.''

''And maybe you're not telling me everything.''

I didn't reply to that. Instead, I asked, "Am I being charged with something?"

Gannon rubbed his jaw, leaning back in his chair. A lock of his wavy hair had tumbled over his forehead. I thought again how much he looked like John Wayne. He even had the lazy drawl.

"I'm going to take your word this time about somebody doctoring your drink, as crazy as it sounds. Just remember what I told you before—I don't like private investigators. If you're withholding evidence, I'm going to come down on you hard, Kate McHaney. Now, would you like to go across the street with me for some breakfast?"

I blinked with surprise. "One minute you're telling me how much you don't like private detectives, and the next breath you're inviting me to breakfast. What is it with you, Sheriff?"

He shrugged. "It's nothing personal. I don't like private eyes in general. Oh . . . and they make real good scrambled eggs across the street."

I managed a weak smile. "Okay."

At the restaurant, I went into the women's rest room. I looked like death warmed over. I splashed cold water on my face and ran a comb through my hair. It didn't help much.

I returned to the booth, where Steve Gannon was seated before two cups of steaming coffee.

After last night I didn't think I'd ever trust a cup of coffee again, but this was delicious. "How about my truck?"

"It's okay. We brought it in. It's parked behind the courthouse."

"Was it banged up much?"

"I don't know. How can you tell?"

"I guess you have a point there."

He took a sip of his coffee. "Do you live around here?"

"I have a houseboat on the Intercoastal Canal, south of Brownsville."

He gave me an amused, surprised look. "You live on a houseboat?"

"Yes."

"Alone?"

"I have a dog named Bismark."

He chuckled, shaking his head. "A houseboat. That must be fun."

It was the first time I'd seen his serious, stern expression relax. I was being treated to a human side of Sheriff Steve Gannon. It was quite attractive.

"Yes," I said, "I can fish off my front porch."

"I'd like that." He almost sounded wistful.

The eggs came. They were, as Steve had promised, delicious. I was starting to feel more human by the minute. As I ate, I stole glances at the sheriff. *Oh, no*, I thought, *I'm having some very unsettling feelings about this man.*

I decided I might as well go for broke. "Got a family?" I asked. *Good grief! Surely I'm not blushing*, I thought, horrified. My cheeks did feel warm.

"A son," he said. "He's five."

I waited.

"His mother and I are separated," he added.

Separated? As in temporary estrangement? Pending divorce? He didn't elaborate.

"Well," I said right out, brazen hussy that I am, "you'll have to bring your son down to fish off my front porch sometime."

He gave me his slow, John Wayne smile. "Well, y'know, he'd like that, and so would I. Thanks."

Gee, I thought, *we've gone all the way from his throwing me in jail for drug abuse to being friends. What's in store for us next?*

He picked up the check. "Guess I'd better get back to the office," he said without a whole lot of enthusiasm.

"Yes, and I have things to do." (Such as catching a plane to Nashville, Tennessee.)

"Thanks for the breakfast and for believing me about what happened last night." I held out my hand. When he shook it, a tingling feeling went up my arm. It was a nice sensation.

When I got back to my truck, I surveyed the damage. As Steve had said, the trusty old clunker already had so many dents and rust spots that last night's encounter with the Bronco hardly detracted from the resale value.

I hurried back to the houseboat, took a warm bath, dressed in comfortable traveling clothes—a white blouse and tan slacks—tossed a few necessary items into an overnight bag, called Catfish Charlie to ask him to feed Bismark tonight, and then I was on my way to the airport.

From the valley, I took a flight to Houston, where I changed to the plane that would take me to Nashville. During the flight I had plenty of time to go back over last night's events. This case had taken on an ugly twist. Now the killer who had murdered three of Freddie's musicians was after me. The thought put a queasy feeling in the pit of my stomach. If I had any sense, I would turn what I knew over to Steve Gannon and tell Freddie I was resigning from the case. But I couldn't bring myself to do that without first solving the mystery of Lorraine's past. She was the clue to this whole thing. Getting some answers about her might save Freddie's life as well as my own.

I reviewed last night's guest list. Whoever put the knockout drops in the coffee hoped I'd pass out on the way home and have a fatal accident. The most obvious person to suspect was Lorraine. She had caught me snooping in her bedroom. She had suggested that I get a cup of coffee from Manuel, the bartender.

But there was the matter of that Bronco that had dogged me on the road, almost forcing me into the ditch. Was that part of the plan, or was it a coincidence? Was Lorraine capable of that kind of reckless driving?

When my plane landed in Nashville, I rented the most inexpensive compact car available. I bought a city map at the magazine counter in the terminal. Using the map, I easily located the address given on the driver's license made out to Lorraine when she was going under the name of Madeline Smith. It turned out to be a modest apartment complex.

The apartment manager was an agreeable man. I gave him my business card and explained I was a private investigator trying to locate a former tenant, Madeline Smith. He chuckled. "Wonder what that lady's been up to? You're the second person in the last two weeks who's been in here looking for her."

I felt a shiver run up my spine. "Was it a sandy-haired, one-armed man?"

"Sure was. You know him?"

"No," I said, but I sure wished I did. The mysterious one-armed man, whoever he was, was consistently two weeks ahead of me in my search for the real Lorraine Landers. Who was he, and what was he looking for?

As the apartment manager checked back through his records, he said that he remembered he couldn't find a Madeline Smith, but he did locate a lease made out to a Mr. and Mrs. Taylor Smith. The lease showed that they had lived in the apartment for about a year.

The manager elaborated, "I remember the husband, Taylor Smith, died a little over a year ago. His wife stayed on a couple of months, then moved out. The file doesn't show that she gave any forwarding address."

I showed him Lorraine's picture, but he couldn't be sure she was the Mrs. Smith who rented from him. That was understandable since she had looked quite different then with dark hair.

"Did she have any friends? Anyone who might remember her?"

"Well," he said, thumbing through the lease papers, "we have tenants fill out information forms giving references, places of employment, stuff like that. You wouldn't believe how many renters will bust up the place and then skip out owing rent. One guy stole the toilet out of his apartment. If we have a record of references and where they work, we can sometimes take legal action. Now, according to this file, Mrs. Smith was employed at the Buena Vista Nursing Home."

"That could be helpful. Do you have the address?"

"Yes, ma'am." He obligingly wrote the address on a scrap of paper and then showed me on my city map the easiest way to reach the place.

I was batting a thousand. At the Buena Vista Nursing Home, I found a nurse who had worked with Madeline Smith and knew her quite well. She was a large, cheerful woman named Marjorie Brown. "Sure, I knew Madeline.

We worked the evening shift together for nearly a year. She was a real hard worker. Smart too.''

"Was she a nurse?''

"Well, she wasn't an RN, if that's what you mean. She was a practical nurse, like me.'' She looked at me suspiciously. "Why are you askin' all these questions about Madeline, anyway? You a police officer or something?''

I ran a quick search through my mental computer and trotted out the name I had seen on the letter in Lorraine's purse. "A friend of Madeline's from Sandersville, her hometown in North Carolina, asked me to check on her while I was in Nashville. Did Madeline ever mention Donna to you?''

"Oh, Donna Compton! Sure she did. She spoke of Donna a lot. They grew up together. You a friend of Donna's?''

"Well, I know her. When she heard I was coming to Nashville, she asked me to ask about Madeline. Said she hadn't heard from her in quite a while.''

Marjorie nodded sadly. "Poor Madeline was pretty broke up when her husband died. Said she was goin' to leave and start life over somewhere. Guess she just quit writing folks back home. I never heard from her either after she left.''

"Was she married long?''

" 'Bout a year, I guess. It was so sad. They made such a good-looking couple.''

"What did her husband do?''

"Taylor? He was a country-western musician. Played guitar with some pretty well-known groups around here.''

Something like a lot of cold little pinpricks ran up the back of my neck. I really didn't want to hear this, but I had to ask. "That's really sad,'' I said sympathetically. I took a breath and asked, "What happened to Taylor?''

"Some kind of food poisoning, I heard. Came on suddenly after a party they gave for some musician friends."

The cold, queasy lump was back in the pit of my stomach.

"Poor Madeline," I said sadly. "Donna will be real sorry to hear about that. I don't guess there was any life insurance—"

"Well, yeah, I do believe Taylor had taken out some sizable insurance."

"That's nice," I murmured. "At least poor Madeline wasn't left penniless."

"Yes. Tell Donna they had a real nice memorial service for Taylor."

"Yes, I will. Is Taylor buried here in Nashville?"

"I believe Madeline said he was cremated."

That Madeline, I thought. *What a practical woman.*

From the nursing home I drove to a filling station where I gassed up the rented compact and bought a road map. I saw that Interstate 40 could have me in North Carolina by nightfall. My destination, Sandersville, however, was on the other side of Asheville and could only be reached by a winding state road. I had the chilling feeling that Freddie Landers's time was running out, but I was not about to drive through those North Carolina mountains in the dark.

I spent the night in a Motel Six just inside North Carolina. Early the next morning, I set out for Sandersville. This was back-country North Carolina. It was a beautiful, scenic drive if you didn't mind hairpin turns, rickety bridges with barely room for two cars to squeeze by, and sheer drops of hundreds of feet off the side of the narrow pavement.

My ears popped as I climbed steadily upward, driving through what looked like patches of fog but were actually low-hanging clouds. I went by sheds where broad tobacco leaves were drying. I saw bright-colored hand-stitched quilts hung out for sale on split-rail fences in front of unpainted frame cabins.

I reached Sandersville early in the afternoon. It was a small, isolated mountain town that probably had not changed much since Stonewall Jackson's army camped here on the way to fight the Yankees. In the center of town was a statue of a Confederate soldier standing guard beside a rusty cannon.

I had no trouble finding the address I had seen on the envelopes in Lorraine's purse. It was a modest two-bedroom frame house with blue shutters and beds of flowers in the front yard. The woman who came to the door said she was Donna's mother. Why was I not surprised when she told me Donna was at work at the nursing home on Elm Street?

I went to the nursing home on Elm Street. Donna was the receptionist, a plump, plain, pleasant woman about Lorraine's age. When I told her I was from Texas, where I'd met her friend Madeline, she became quite upset and burst into tears.

"I've spent the last year wondering why Madeline treated me this way," she sobbed, dabbing at her streaming eyes with a wad of tissues. "We grew up together. We were best friends all through school. We worked here at the nursing home for years. We wrote regularly when she moved to Nashville after Ken died. Then suddenly my letters started coming back marked 'Moved, No Forwarding Address.' I've been so worried and so upset. How is Madeline? Is she all right?"

"Yes, she's fine. She asked me to look you up and tell you that she's fine and she's sorry that she hasn't written. Who's Ken?"

"Ken—her husband. Didn't she ever speak about him?"

"Well, I don't know her that well."

"I can understand," Donna said, patting her streaked mascara. "It was such a shock, losing him that way. Listen, it's time for my coffee break. Come on; I want to hear all about Madeline."

She propelled me across the street to the town's only café, taking along a box of tissues in case talking about Madeline brought a fresh flood of tears. She ordered coffee and I asked for a Coke.

"Madeline and I grew up as close as sisters," Donna said. "She had such a hard childhood, her mother dying so young and her father—well, you know." She pantomimed raising a shot glass to her lips while giving me a knowing look. "Whenever he was on one of his binges, Madeline stayed at our house. He got real mean when he was drinking. Never could hold a job. It broke my heart to see some of the old clothes Madeline had to wear to school. But she held her head high in spite of the way kids made fun of her. She was smart, and she had determination and ambition. I don't know how many times she told me, 'Donna, I'm going to be rich someday. I'm going to live in a big house and drive a big car, and nothing and nobody's going to stop me.' "

Donna sniffled into some of the tissues, then leaned forward eagerly. "Tell me how she is, please."

I thought about Lorraine's red Cadillac, the designer clothes filling a closet big enough to rent out as an efficiency apartment, and Freddie's swimming pool in the shape of a guitar. "Well, I guess you could say her ambitions came true," I told Donna honestly. "She's living in a big house and driving a big car. She's married to a very wealthy Texan.''

That bit of information used up some more of Donna's supply of tissues as she wept for joy. "I'm so glad that it all turned out so well for her. She and poor Ken just weren't right for each other. Ken was sweet, but he didn't have ambition the way Madeline did. He would have been perfectly happy to spend the rest of his life right here in Sandersville.''

"Tell me about Ken.''

"Madeline and Ken started going together when she was in high school. They dated off and on for years. Ken kept wanting them to get married, but Madeline put him off. I think she was hoping for a better offer, but there isn't much choice in a town this size. Finally, she gave in and they got married. Ken was a musician. Played fiddle. Best country-western fiddler in this part of the state. 'Course, you don't get rich doing that.''

I dreaded asking the next question. "What happened?''

"It was horrible. Ken fell asleep at the wheel, driving up to Hendersonville to play at the Moose Lodge. It was early too. He and Madeline had just had supper before he left. It wasn't as if he was coming back late after a job. I guess he was just overly tired. He went over that bad curve this side of Parker's Crossing. It's a sheer drop. His car caught fire when it crashed at the bottom.'' She added in a hushed tone, "They had to have a closed-casket funeral.''

I knew what the answer to my next question was going to be, but I had to ask anyway. "Must have been hard on poor Madeline, the funeral expenses and all. . . .''

"Well, fortunately, Madeline had insisted that Ken carry a pretty fair amount of life insurance—''

I got to a telephone as fast as I could extricate myself from Donna's tearful presence. I put in a call to Sheriff Steve Gannon. When he came on the line, he said, "Kate? Where in the world are you?"

"North Carolina."

"North Carolina!" he said incredulously.

"Steve, I don't have time to do a lot of explaining. I'll give you all the details when I get back. The reason I'm calling is to tell you to find Freddie Landers right away. I have found out some very scary things about Madeline Smith."

"Wait a minute. Who is Madeline Smith?"

"I'm sorry. Lorraine. Freddie's wife. Madeline Smith was one of the names she used. Steve, you have to warn Freddie to get away from that woman right away. She's a killer. She's probably psycho. Take my word for it, you have to get Freddie away from her before it's too late—"

Sheriff Gannon's voice was stern. "Kate McHaney, you get yourself back here as fast as you can. You may be facing a serious charge of withholding evidence and obstructing justice. Lorraine Landers has been kidnapped."

Chapter Seven

Lorraine kidnapped? I was stunned. This was a totally unexpected development, but I didn't have time to deal with it then.

I drove immediately to Asheville, where I returned the car to the rental-agency branch in that city. Flight connections went smoothly. I was back in the Rio Grande valley airport by dark.

It was Saturday night. As soon as the plane landed, I put in a call to Steve Gannon. He was not in his office. I left the message with a deputy that I was back and would try to reach him later.

On the way home, I stopped at my office to check the mail and my answering machine. I saw that the mail contained nothing urgent and shoved it in a desk drawer. The answering machine contained a number of calls from Steve made earlier in the day, each one sounding more angry and frustrated than the one before.

I drove home feeling tired and gritty from the long trip. Bismark greeted me ecstatically. "I'm glad to see you, too, fella," I said wearily. At the moment, the most urgent need in my life was a warm shower. I shucked my clothes on the way to the bathroom.

The shower felt so good, I was considering spending the night there when Bismark set up a ferocious racket outside. I turned off the shower, shrugged into a terry-cloth robe, and hurried to the front door.

Bismark had Steve Gannon cornered on the deck of the houseboat. The dog was snarling and barking furiously. Steve looked mad enough to pull his gun.

I flipped on a light that flooded the deck and at the same time I pressed two fingers against my tongue and gave a shrill whistle.

Bismark obediently trotted to my side.

Steve glared at me. "I ought to have animal control pick up that vicious beast."

"I believe you were trespassing, Sheriff," I said coldly. "He was just doing what he's been trained to do, guard the premises."

"What kind of dog is he, anyway?"

"Search me."

"He's big as a calf."

Steve took a cautious step toward me. Bismark emitted a low growl. I patted him. "It's all right, honey. He's a friend—sort of." To Steve, I said, "You can come on. He won't bother you now. Shake hands with the nice man, Bismark."

He gave a soft whimper, sat down, and raised a paw obediently. Steve gave him a distrustful glance and made a wide detour around him. I opened the door so Steve could enter.

He gave my living quarters a brief survey. His gaze was

stopped for a moment by the barber chair. Looking at it, he started to say something. He changed his mind and instead murmured, "My deputy relayed your phone message to my radio." He was still staring at the barber chair.

"How did you find where I lived?"

"Just asked. There aren't that many young women living around here alone on a houseboat." He turned his gaze to me. His eyes became intense. I suddenly felt warm.

Steve sounded gruff, but I had the distinct feeling he was very much aware of our isolation here together, just the two of us here on the houseboat. I was self-consciously aware of that too, in a way that made my heart beat faster. His gaze kept sliding away, then returning to me. He was beginning to look flushed, although it was cool that time of the evening with the night breeze coming off the water.

I made an effort to regain some composure. "I was stunned to hear that Lorraine had been kidnapped. What in the world happened?"

He was brief. "This morning about ten o'clock, we got a call from the Landers's maid. She sounded hysterical. Said she'd heard loud voices and a struggle up in Lorraine's room. A few minutes later, she caught sight of someone dragging Lorraine out to a car.

"We sent a deputy out right away," he continued. "There were signs of a violent struggle in her room. The maid isn't much help. She can't give us a description of the man who dragged Lorraine out to the car or the kind of car he was driving. She was so hysterical she can't even remember for sure what color it was."

"How about the security guard Freddie keeps at the front gate?"

"He wasn't around. Freddie had taken him along to where they're shooting that movie. He's Freddie's bodyguard."

"Oh, yeah. I remember Freddie telling me at the party Thursday night that he was leaving early the next morning with the movie company to shoot some scenes in a border town. He said he'd be there several days. Did the kidnapper leave a message?"

"No."

"Have you heard anything from him—any ransom demands, stuff like that?"

"No. Not a word, yet."

I frowned. "Have you considered it might be a homicide rather than a kidnapping?"

"Of course. But for the time being, we're treating it as a kidnapping. Freddie Landers is a wealthy man, a good target for a hefty kidnapping ransom demand."

I had an ominous feeling. There was something about this kidnapping that was altogether out of kilter in the context of the things I had been finding out about Lorraine Landers, alias Madeline Smith. My gut instinct was that Lorraine's disappearance had nothing to do with money, but I couldn't tell you why I felt that way.

Steve said severely, "Now you start talking, Kate McHaney. I know you've been snooping around in Freddie's and Lorraine's private affairs. I have the distinct feeling you haven't told me everything you've found out, and that has the smell of obstructing justice, something which can get your private investigator's license jerked and maybe land you in the slammer to boot. What were you doing in North Carolina anyway?"

"Calm down, will you?" I retorted, my temper beginning to heat up. "I have plenty to tell you. You don't have to come around here with your big, tough cop attitude. Look, I haven't had anything to eat since breakfast. Is it all right if we have a snack while we talk? I'm famished.''

He was momentarily caught off guard. He had come charging in here, all primed to give me a scorching interrogation. Instead, here I stood before him, just out of a shower, probably looking pretty sexy with my hair damp and disheveled and the robe clinging to me, suggesting we turn the situation into a sociable meal.

Well, to make it even, I was being caught equally off guard. Ever since meeting Sheriff Steve Gannon, my defenses had been in a state of disarray. My past experiences with men had not been all that great. I don't guess I'd ever been in love for real. The few experiences I'd had with guys back home had convinced me a lot of guys are rats. Anyway, I had left New York to start a new life. Men had been at the very bottom of my list of priorities. All of my energies had gone into making a success of my business and my new life.

Now this big, rangy, broad-shouldered Texan in his neatly pressed sheriff's khakis, who gave his marital status vaguely as ''separated,'' was in my houseboat stirring up feelings that I did not want to deal with.

I made a fast retreat to the refrigerator, which yielded up several varieties of cheese, fresh cold fruit, and a bottle of chilled white wine. I found an avocado and quickly put together a guacamole salad. I arranged the meal on the card table I used for dining purposes.

Steve stood watching me awkwardly. I opened a folding chair, which I placed on the opposite side of the table.

''I owe you a meal,'' I said.

''Meal?''

"Breakfast yesterday. The scrambled eggs. After I spent the night in your jail."

"Oh, yeah."

I thought of mentioning suing him for false arrest, but decided under the circumstances it might be as well to let sleeping dogs lie. We ate in silence. I devoured several slices of Swiss cheese with crackers and had a glass of wine. Then I had a slice of cold mango that was ripe enough to be deliciously sweet. Steve, I noticed, was having several helpings of my guacamole salad.

The entire time, the awareness between us was acute, like electricity sizzling in the night air. Steve tried not to be obvious about it, but from time to time he looked at me in an intense way. It was a look that angered and excited me. I think it angered me *because* it excited me.

The silence was becoming so brittle it was about to explode like shattering plate glass. I had to say something, *anything.* "So, Lorraine Landers has been kidnapped—or something. That lady has been leading a very eventful life."

Steve cleared his throat, dismissing whatever fantasies were no doubt occupying his mind. He scowled and became all business again. "That's what I want you to tell me about. And this time, don't leave anything out."

"Have some more salad."

"Yes, thanks. It's very good."

I refilled our wineglasses. "To begin with, Lorraine sounded fishy to me. The story she told Freddie about coming from a wealthy family in Rio Dulce was pure fiction. I found out her real name is Madeline Smith. Her last residence before coming here was Nashville, Tennessee. Now get this: While living in Nashville, she was married for a short while to a country-western musician who died of food poisoning after eating a meal she served up, leaving her a sizable life-insurance policy. She prudently had the remains cremated.

"Before moving to Nashville," I continued, "she lived in Sandersville, North Carolina, where she was married to a country-western fiddle player who mysteriously fell asleep behind the wheel shortly after she fed him supper one night. He drove off one of those North Carolina mountainsides. He was burned to a cinder when his car crashed. She'd also seen to it that he carried life insurance. So you can see why I immediately put in that call to you to warn Freddie that he is apparently married to some kind of black-widow spider.

"From what I learned through Donna Compton, a lifelong friend of Lorraine Landers—or Madeline, to use her real name—Lorraine is a very ambitious woman. Driven, you might say. For some reason, she picks country-western musicians to marry.

"She started at the bottom of the heap with a local fiddle player, cashed in his modest life insurance, moved up a notch to a better-known musician in Nashville and got a bigger chunk of life insurance. Then she must have decided to move into the big time. She picked nationally known Freddie Landers as husband number three, moved down here, contrived to meet him, and now plans to inherit his worldly possessions, including a million-dollar life-insurance policy. The food poisoning he complained about and the short in his electric wiring were failed attempts to do him in."

Steve listened, poker-faced.

"You don't buy it," I said disgustedly.

"Stop being so defensive. I didn't say that. It sounds

plausible, though hard to prove with her first husband burned to a cinder in the car wreck and the second cremated.''

"True, but you can't write this off as coincidence. Two husbands, both country-western musicians, both dead within a year or so of marrying her, both with life insurance. Now husband number three, big-name country-western, rock-music star.''

Steve nodded.

"The other strange coincidences, the three musicians from Freddie's band dying within a few months of one another, must tie in with all of this somehow, but I haven't figured that one out.''

"Well,'' Steve said, "this is all a bunch of fine speculation, but my job right now is to find out who kidnapped Lorraine.''

"Since you consider the possibility of its being a kidnapping, I assume the FBI has been called in.''

Steve nodded.

I toyed thoughtfully with my wineglass. "There's one more thing. I haven't the foggiest notion how it fits in, but apparently somebody else has been interested in Lorraine's past. Almost everywhere I checked, I was told that a guy had been there about two weeks ahead of me asking questions about Lorraine. The description I got was a middle-aged man, sandy hair, with one arm.''

"Hmm. That's interesting.''

"Know any one-armed men around here?''

"Yes. Several.''

"Maybe one of them is the kidnapper.''

"Maybe.''

We arose from the table. Although I wasn't looking at him, I could feel Steve's attention as I took the wineglasses over to the sink. When I looked over at him, he was studying my old barber chair, but from the flush on his face, I could see it wasn't the chair that really interested him.

He cleared his throat. "I've been meaning to ask. What are you doing with a barber chair?"

"I do haircuts on the side."

He gave me a peculiar look.

"Only joking. I found it in a junk shop. It makes a great reading chair. Want to try it?"

"Some other time."

We started to the door.

"Steve, I've had a lot of experience in finding people. My dog, Bismark, is trained to pick up human scent. Let us see if we can help find Lorraine."

"No."

"What do you mean, 'no'?" I demanded.

"I mean I don't want a private detective nosing around getting in the way. My department and the FBI are quite able to handle this."

I didn't argue the matter with him. I knew how stubborn he could be. But I planned to take Bismark over to Freddie's place in the morning in spite of Sheriff Steve Gannon.

We were standing near the door. The tension between us was back again. It was almost unbearable.

Steve looked down at me. He had that intense look in his eyes again. He said something like, "Thanks for the meal," and I said something like, "You're welcome," although I don't think either one of us really knew what we said.

Then, with a low exclamation, he swept me up in his arms and our lips met. It was like the contact of high-voltage electrical current.

The kiss left my knees feeling like water. Steve, too, was obviously shaken.

I gulped in some air and said shakily, "What's this 'separation' stuff? Do you or don't you have a wife? Are you or aren't you married? I want to know what I'm getting into here."

He looked very troubled. "It's a long story. I'll tell you all about it next time I see you."

Then he slammed out the screen door and crossed the deck in a few long-legged strides. It was almost as if he were running away. Bismark watched him depart with interest but no animosity since I had given him clearance.

I leaned weakly against the doorjamb, all the strength drained from my limbs. I wondered what kind of a complicated entanglement I was getting myself into now.

The next morning, I was up early and drove to my office with Bismark riding in the bed of my pickup. He loved it back there with the wind blowing hard in his face and his tongue hanging out.

On my computer, I typed up a report of my activities and what I had found out about Lorraine. I ran off two copies on my printer. I totaled up the time I had spent on the case and listed my expenses. On my photocopy machine, I made copies of the receipts for the plane fare, car rental, meals, and one-night motel charge. I put all this material in an envelope, sealed it, and wrote Freddie's name on the front.

I then drove to Freddie's ranch, arriving about midmorning. There was no guard at the front gate, but when I pulled up to the big house, I saw a county car with a deputy's insignia and two other dark sedans that looked like FBI to me. There appeared to be a lot of activity going on in the house. I wondered if they'd heard from the kidnappers.

I told Bismark to stay in the truck and got out. Immediately, a man I didn't know appeared at the front door and came down the stairs to check me out. His scrutiny was thorough. He certainly wasn't one of Steve's deputies. I thought he had to be FBI.

"Hello," I said. "My name is Kate McHaney. I came to see Freddie."

"Are you a relative?"

"A friend. Sort of. If you'll give him my name, I'm sure he'll want to see me."

I couldn't see any reason, at the moment, to complicate matters by identifying myself as a private investigator.

"Wait here, please."

He disappeared into the house for a few minutes, then returned and invited me into the house. He led me into a downstairs room that looked like the library and said, "You can talk to Mr. Landers in here."

Freddie appeared presently, looking as if he'd been through the mill. He was haggard, his face drawn, his eyes bleary. He was dressed in his usual Western attire: black trousers, fancy tooled-leather boots, white shirt with fancy stitching, string necktie held together at the neck with a Morgan silver-dollar ornament. His clothes were rumpled, as if he'd slept in them. Even his long, dark mustache seemed to droop more than normal, adding to the overall look of weariness.

" 'Mornin', Miss McHaney," he said with a sigh.

"Good morning, Freddie. Have you heard anything from the kidnappers yet?"

He shook his head. "Not a word. They got the FBI and

everything here. Got all kinds of telephones set up, but we haven't heard a thing. Lorraine has just disappeared into thin air.''

I handed Freddie the envelope. ''It has my report on what I found out the last two days in Tennessee and North Carolina along with an accounting of my expenses and my bill.''

He accepted the envelope and sat heavily in a chair. I took a place on the couch. I felt like a crumb, coming here at a time like this, but it was what he'd paid me to find out. He already knew what the envelope contained, of course. Numbly he said, ''Sheriff Gannon came by late last night and told me what you'd found out about Lorraine.''

''Yes, I had to tell him everything as soon as I got back, Freddie. I'm sorry I wasn't able to talk to you first, but under the circumstances, I would be breaking the law if I withheld any information pertaining to the case.''

He nodded. ''I understand. I'll get a check made out for your bill sometime today.''

''That's all right. No hurry.''

He sat, hands clasped between his knees, shoulders slumped, staring down at the floor, slowly shaking his head. There were tears in his eyes. His face had an unhealthy pallor. ''I just knew there was something wrong about Lorraine,'' he said huskily. ''I've felt it in my bones, deep down for some time, but I didn't want to face up to it. I loved her too much to want it to be true. But it is true.'' He raised his pain-filled gaze to my face. ''She was planning to kill me the way she did her first two husbands, wasn't she?''

''Kind of looks that way,'' I had to admit.

''Do you reckon all of this has anything to do with her kidnapping?''

"I honestly don't know. That has me completely baf-fled."

"I was down on the border with the movie camera crew when it happened," he said. "They called me and I came right home."

"Freddie, I've had special training in finding people. Do you want me to see if I can help locate Lorraine? I don't want to make any rash promises, but there have been some cases where I've succeeded after police were stumped. I won't charge you for my time."

He looked grateful. "I would appreciate that. Even if Lorraine was planning to murder me, I want to know what happened to her."

The poor guy, I thought. *He's still in love with her. He's probably clinging to some forlorn hope that if we can find her, maybe by some miracle she can explain everything that happened in Nashville and North Carolina, convince every-one she didn't murder anyone and wasn't planning to mur-der him. Shakespeare hit the nail on the head when he said love makes fools of us all.*

I patted Freddie's hand, assuring him I'd do all I could to help. Then I left.

I was getting in my pickup when Steve drove up. He came over, looking like a thundercloud. "Kate, what are you doing here? I thought I told you to keep out of this business."

"It's a free country, Sheriff," I said, giving him an impudent grin. "I just came by to give Freddie my report and my bill."

Steve was leaning on the sill of my pickup window, giving me an intense look, kind of a cross between wanting to bawl me out and wanting to kiss me.

Looking at him, I thought what a good-looking hunk of manhood he was. I leaned closer until our lips were inches apart. "Last night was fun," I said in a low, intimate murmur. "We'll have to do it again sometime."

He moved quickly to close the distance between our lips, but I moved faster, drawing back, flipping the key to start my engine. "See you, Sheriff," I said with a grin. Then I took off. I glanced in my rearview mirror and saw him standing spraddle legged in the road, fists on his hips, saying something probably not fit for the ears of women and children.

I put thoughts of Sheriff Steve Gannon out of my mind, replacing them with the ugly matter of Lorraine's abduction. My bad feeling about this whole matter persisted. I didn't believe it was a kidnapping, and I didn't think Steve really believed that either.

I drove slowly down the lane that led from the Landers house to the farm-to-market road outside their gate. Their private hard-topped road inside the property was about a half mile in length. Everyone assumed, I supposed, that the kidnapper had thrown Lorraine into his car and sped at top speed out of the ranch, turned onto the public road, and headed for parts unknown. That would be the natural assumption.

I have a suspicious nature about things happening in ways that seem obvious. The ugly suspicions I was having about this case kept me searching the area as I drove. This ranch property of Freddie's was not big by the usual standard of Texas ranches. It did, however, cover a lot of acres. It stretched off in both directions from the private road as far as you could see. Some of it was open grazing pasture, but there were wooded areas, thickets of mesquite, huisache, and other native trees and bushes. Plenty of places to hide a person.

About midway to the gate, I saw what looked like car tracks off the side of the road. The ground was hard-packed here, so I couldn't be sure. I stopped anyway, parked off the road, and whistled for Bismark. He happily jumped down from the bed of the truck and joined me.

Looking more closely, I saw that there were tire tracks going from the lane, across an area of grazing land. It hadn't rained in some time. The ground was so hard, the car tracks were barely visible. There was no telling if they were a day, a week, or a month old. I set out on foot, following their general direction, anyway.

I put Bismark on alert with the signal he'd been trained to recognize: "Bismark—go find!"

Immediately, he became excited, running off in all directions, sniffing the air.

It takes a year or more to train an air-scent dog. They are not what most people think of as tracking dogs like bloodhounds. Those tracking dogs smell an article containing the scent of the person they're trying to find, then go off trying to pick up and follow that particular scent. Bloodhounds are used by posses to track escaped convicts.

Air-scent dogs used by search-and-find experts have a different kind of training. They are used to find a lost person, such as a child in a wilderness area. They pick up and follow the scent that is caused by countless dead skin cells shed every minute by the human body. This scent is carried by air currents for long distances. Even if the lost person is dead, trained air-scent dogs can still pick up his trail. The ability of these dogs is uncanny. They can pick up human scents that are days, sometimes weeks, old, from distances of a half mile and more.

Since the dog is not hunting for a particular scent, it may not locate any particular individual, but a dog can help a searcher determine if a human has been in the area. Often what the dog locates will turn out to be a false lead. But there are other times when the dog leads the searcher straight to the lost victim.

Following the faint car tracks, Bismark and I wandered along for a mile or more across the open prairie. The dog didn't show any sign of picking up any smell.

It was getting close to noon. The midday Texas sun was giving me a fierce roasting. I was perspiring freely. Flies were swarming around me. I was plodding over the dry, sun-baked earth, getting a blister on my heel and beginning to feel very foolish. If someone had brought Lorraine out here, killed her, and left her body anywhere in the area, there would be buzzards circling above us. There wasn't a buzzard in the sky.

Then Bismark suddenly went on alert. I knew the signs immediately. He stopped running in random circles. His head jerked up, and he began moving forward in a straight, purposeful manner. He had picked up a human scent.

I forgot the heat and discomfort. Bismark led me toward a clump of trees. It was an area wooded with thorny native trees around a caliche pit filled with water. Cattle trails through the undergrowth leading to the pit showed that it was used as a watering tank. Caliche is a type of clay used for things like topping roads. At one time, the clay had been dug from here, leaving a pit ten or twenty feet deep. In time it had filled with rainwater, forming a small lake.

Bismark ran straight to the water's edge, barking now

with frantic excitement. He suddenly jumped into the pond and swam to the other side where he climbed out, shaking water from his coat. He looked across the tank at me, barking, then plunged in and swam back. When he climbed out, he again shook, sending a shower of spray over me. It was obvious to me he was still on strong alert.

I had a clammy sensation between my shoulder blades. I was pretty sure we had found Lorraine.

I rewarded Bismark with praise, then returned to the pickup and drove back to Freddie's house. Steve and one of his deputies were in the yard. I got out of my pickup and walked over to them. I said, "I think you'd better drag the old caliche watering tank. I think you'll find Lorraine."

Steve stared at me.

"I had Bismark search the area. He caught scent of somebody in the water," I continued.

Steve's deputy, overhearing me, gave a derisive snort. "Can't no dog smell a body that's under the water."

"Wait a minute," Steve said. "It's true. I've read about trained air-scent dogs used by search-and-rescue people. The dogs can catch the scent of a body in the water. The scent rises to the surface. Is your dog that well trained?"

"You'd better believe it."

Steve had a boat and dragging equipment taken to the pond. About midafternoon, they brought up Lorraine. Concrete blocks had been tied to her legs.

She had been strangled with one of Freddie's wide Western belts. It was still around her throat.

Chapter Eight

G oing to a funeral is not my idea of a fun way to spend an afternoon, but I felt obligated to attend the last rites for Lorraine.

The event was impressive. Lorraine was laid to rest amid a mountain of flowers. Professional singers were flown in from Nashville to provide a choir. I estimated that the casket cost as much as a Mercedes. The crowd was huge. The service was conducted by a nationally known television evangelist.

The job the undertaker did on Lorraine can only be described as a work of art. She looked even more glamorous in death than she had in life. Her features were composed, her cheeks flushed, her hair expertly styled. I remembered her appearance the last time I'd seen her, when they dragged her out of the water—hair bedraggled and muddy, face a pasty white. And around her neck had been that dreadful belt that strangled the life out of her.

Freddie baffled me. He had obviously spent a fortune to send Lorraine off in style. He was dressed in a black Western outfit, and he looked sincerely bereaved. Had he forgotten that Lorraine might have been plotting to murder him?

Looking very broad-shouldered and handsome in a dark suit and polished boots, Steve was present at the funeral service. I tried unsuccessfully to stop stealing glances at him. *Who are you trying to fool, Kate?* I thought. *You've gone and done it. You've got yourself hooked on this big, good-looking Texan. Now what?*

When the procession arrived at the cemetery, a magnetic force over which I had little control caused me to drift to his side. Steve hadn't spoken to me since Bismark found Lorraine's body. He'd warned me to keep my nose out of the affair, and then I'd embarrassed the sheriff's department and the FBI by finding the missing victim practically under their noses. I had the feeling that Steve was not very happy with me.

"Quite a show," I ventured.

His reply was cool. "Freddie can well afford it. He stands to collect a million dollars on Lorraine's life insurance."

I looked up at him curiously, wondering what was going through his mind. Surely he couldn't suspect Freddie, who had an ironclad alibi. At the time Lorraine had been dragged out of the house by her unknown assailant, Freddie was miles away at the border town, on location with the movie crew.

Steve and I were standing under some trees on the outer fringes of the mourners. "Mourners" is a term I use loosely. I saw many who had been at the fiesta on Freddie's ranch. I had serious doubts they were shedding any tears. Among those present were movie director Max Brice, Freddie's cousin and recording studio owner Milton Bowman, and land developer Sam Tompkins. I didn't recall any of them exhibiting much fondness for Lorraine.

It was quite possible, I thought, that I was rubbing shoulders with Lorraine's murderer. For example, Sam Tompkins had made it clear that he resented Lorraine, resented the fact that she had taken over Freddie's business operations and was cutting him out of some juicy real-estate deals in the theme-park venture. He was probably delighted to have her out of the way. Then there was the business manager Lorraine had fired, Kenneth Mayfield. Tompkins had mentioned him. I hadn't met him so I didn't know if he was at the funeral, but he must have hated Lorraine for firing him. Hated her enough to kill her?

Who else might have murdered Lorraine?

Oh, yeah, the mysterious one-armed man who kept turning up one jump ahead of me during my investigation of Lorraine. Who was he? What part did he play in her life? Did he have a motive for murdering her?

Or had it just been a random intruder? The autopsy had shown that Lorraine was not sexually molested. There were a lot of nuts running around these days breaking and entering to steal something for drug money. Nothing was missing from the house, a fact which had at first caused the sheriff's department to suspect kidnapping. But Lorraine might have surprised the intruder before he took anything. He might have panicked, strangled her, and dumped her body in the watering tank.

The fact that the killer knew the location of the watering tank meant it must be a person who had some knowledge of Freddie's ranch. A stranger passing through the area wouldn't have known about that small, artificial lake.

I thought my involvement in the case ended with Lor-

raine's casket being lowered into the grave. I had done what
Freddie Landers hired me to do. I had uncovered Lorraine's
lurid past and thereby found the person who was probably
trying to kill him. Then, when Lorraine was abducted, he'd
asked me to find her, something I had also done. Now there
was nothing left except to type up a final report of the case
for my files.

I guessed wrong. After the funeral, I returned to my office
and spent the next several days with less dramatic work.
Then, one morning, a haggard-looking Freddie Landers appeared at my office. "I need to talk to you," he blurted out
the minute he strode through the doorway.

Today he was wearing a pearl-gray Western suit with the
usual fancy stitching, a lavender shirt, and a black string
tie. My attention was drawn to his wide leather belt with
its ornate gold buckle. He apparently had one for every day
in the week. The belt gave me a chilly shiver, reminding
me of the one that I had seen around Lorraine's throat when
they pulled her out of the water.

Freddie was in some kind of emotional state. He paced
around my office, wringing his hands. "Freddie, calm
down," I ordered. "Have a cup of coffee."

Something about Freddie Landers brought out a maternal
streak in me. He didn't fit the stereotype of the ego-ridden
superstar. The impression he had given me from the first
time we met was that of a good-natured, kind of dumb
country boy who had accidentally stumbled into stardom
and wasn't sure what to make of it. The way Lorraine had
mesmerized him convinced me he wasn't overly bright. I
had the feeling Freddie needed a big sister to protect him.

I poured him a cup of coffee and got him to sit down.
Freddie gulped some of the coffee, then put the cup on

the edge of my desk. It rattled when he sat it down. He removed one of his skinny cigars from his gold case and lit it with an unsteady hand. He puffed on it a few times, then rested his trembling hand, with the cheroot clamped between index and middle finger, on his knee. There was a heavy gold ring on his ring finger and a glittering diamond on his pinky. Smoke wafted upward from his pencil-thin cigar. He stared out my window. Smoke drifted past his eyes. His face was deeply lined. He looked as if he'd aged ten years since Lorraine's death. He appeared tired, deflated, and haunted.

"This thing has me all tore up," he began. "Lorraine was so beautiful, and now she's dead. I can't stop thinking about her."

"In spite of the fact that she might have been planning to kill you, Freddie?"

"I know," he sighed, "but it's hard to figure out how things can be between a man and a woman, Miss McHaney. Sometimes the way a man can make a fool of himself over a woman doesn't make much sense. I know in my mind that the things you found out about Lorraine make her look like a scheming, dangerous woman. But my heart won't listen to reason. She had a hold on me that I can't explain. I loved her so much, I don't want to believe those things. A part of me thinks we don't know for sure she did anything wrong. Maybe if she was alive, she could explain everything."

I thought he should be making a note of what he was saying. It would make great lyrics for his next country-western, crying-in-your-beer song. Maybe he could give it the title "Dumb, Blind in Love." A man would certainly have to be dumb, blind in love not to see Lorraine for what she was.

Then he laid something on me that gave me pause. He said, looking directly at me, "If it was Lorraine who was trying to kill me, how about the three boys in my old band who have been killed this year? You think Lorraine wanted me to die so she'd collect my life insurance. But she didn't have anything against those musicians. She didn't even know them."

I chewed on my lip. I knew something in the back of my mind had been bothering me all along, and this was it. I made an attempt at being logical. "We're not sure those musicians were murdered. The police investigated the deaths pretty thoroughly. And if they were homicides, they might not have been related to the attempts on your life."

Freddie didn't look convinced. I'm not sure I was, either.

"Anyway," he said, "I just can't rest until the person who murdered Lorraine is behind bars. The reason I came over here this morning is to ask you to keep working for me. I want you to find out who killed Lorraine."

I thought the law-enforcement agencies were in a much better position than a lone private investigator to solve a homicide. I tried to convince Freddie of that, but he insisted on retaining me. "You found Lorraine's body when the sheriff and the FBI couldn't," he pointed out.

That was true, I had to admit with some justifiable pride. "I just got lucky," I protested, making a feeble attempt at modesty.

Well, I thought if nothing else, it would give me an excuse to visit Steve. Perhaps I could mend some fences there. Besides, I'd become emotionally involved in this situation. There were too many unanswered questions bothering me.

Who murdered Lorraine and why? Were the musicians from Freddie's band murdered, and if so, why? Was there a connection with those deaths, the attempts on Freddie's life, and Lorraine's murder? Maybe I'd watched too many *Columbo* stories on TV, but I like things answered and logically tied up in a tidy fashion before the ending.

Freddie and I agreed on a new contract and advance. I promised to keep a running-expense account and to call him whenever I had anything to report. Then I turned on my answering machine, locked my office, and drove to the county seat where Steve Gannon held the office of sheriff. I arrived at noon and phoned his office.

"Hi," I said when Steve came on the line.

A moment of strained silence.

"I'd like to buy you lunch," I said.

Peace offering.

He kept me waiting another moment while he thought it over. "All right."

"I'm at Rosita's café across the street from the courthouse."

"Okay. I'll be there in a few minutes."

I selected a corner booth for privacy and waited with jittery feelings not unlike a teenager waiting for an important date. Do any of us ever completely grow up?

The jukebox was playing a twangy Mexican *conjunto* song. The atmosphere was heavy with the mingled odors of refried beans, enchiladas, and beer. Hamburger patties were sizzling on a grill. Behind the counter, a clock outlined with pink neon tubing, with a Lone Star Beer ad on its face, pointed to twelve noon. The midday lunch crowd was settling in.

In due time, Steve arrived, filling the place with his presence. He slid into the booth seat across the table from me. He was wearing his usual sharply creased sheriff's uniform made of gray material with brown trim. The gold sheriff's badge pinned to his right breast pocket looked heavy and official. His sharp gray eyes gave me an intent look. "Hello, Kate." His voice was more cordial than when he'd spoken to me at the funeral, but there was still an air of reserve about him.

"Hello." Good grief, I even sounded breathless.

"You're looking nice."

"Thanks. So are you. I thought you were mad at me."

"I was a little annoyed," he admitted. "I told you not to interfere in the Landers case, and you stubbornly went right ahead anyway. But Bismark did find the body. I have to give you credit for that."

"Bismark found her, but I pointed him in the right direction."

"Don't press your luck." He looked at the menu but seemed to have other things on his mind.

The waitress came to the booth. I ordered a club sandwich and a glass of iced tea. Steve asked for a hamburger and a cup of coffee.

Then there was strained silence again. If he wasn't mad at me, why couldn't he think of anything to say? The reserve was like a wall around him.

I never was one to keep my mouth shut. "You sure act like you're mad at me."

He frowned. His gray eyes filled with some kind of inner conflict. "On the contrary," he said slowly, "I'm anything but angry with you. That's the trouble."

"Steve, you're not making a lot of sense."

"Probably not. You've been causing me some sleepless nights, Kate."

I liked the sound of that. "Oh?" I asked hopefully.

I waited. Apparently this was not easy for him. I tried to help him out by saying the first thing that came to mind: "This maybe has something to do with your wife from whom, I think you said, you're separated?"

Bingo.

"You're very perceptive. We need to talk. But this isn't a very good time or place."

So much for personal matters. Again silence reigned. Lunch arrived. I barely nibbled at my sandwich. I had lost my appetite. *You deserve this for getting involved with a married man*, I told myself. It was beginning to appear that Sheriff Gannon wasn't as separated from his wife as I'd first hoped.

I turned to business. "Do you have any leads on Lorraine's murderer?"

Steve munched his hamburger thoughtfully. He swallowed, took a sip of his coffee, and then said, "Try this. Freddie has the most obvious motive. He and Lorraine have a joint million-dollar life-insurance policy. He suspects Lorraine was trying to knock him off to get the insurance, so he decides to beat her to the punch."

I looked at him incredulously. "You can't seriously consider Freddie a suspect. He was thirty miles away, down on the border with the film company, shooting scenes in the movie about his life."

"Was he?"

"Didn't the cast and the production people see him there?"

Steve took another sip of his coffee. "Yes, he was there

early that morning, filming some scenes. But I talked with
the filming crew. It seems there is a period of time that
Freddie wasn't needed on the set. He told everyone he was
going back to his trailer. For the next hour and a half, he
doesn't have an alibi. Nobody saw him during that time.
Freddie drives a fast sports car, a Jaguar. It wouldn't have
been any great trick for him to have covered the distance
from the movie set to his home in a half hour, strangled
Lorraine, dumped her body in the lake, and made it back
in time for his next appearance on the set.''

"That's very farfetched and circumstantial.''

"Is it? Remember, the murder weapon was one of Freddie's belts.''

"That proves he didn't do it! I'll admit Freddie is sort
of dumb, but surely he would have had better sense than
to leave a belt so easily identified as his around his victim's
neck.''

"Not necessarily. He would have been nervous and in a
big hurry. And he'd wired her to concrete blocks, so he
figured she'd be on the bottom of that lake for years.''

The short fuse on my temper was beginning to sizzle. "I
can't buy it. I know Freddie Landers. I just talked to him
this morning. He is sincerely broken up about Lorraine's
death. In spite of everything, he loved the woman. He
wasn't capable of murdering her. I think you need to make
an arrest in this case, so you're grabbing at straws.''

Now Steve started looking mad. "You aren't poking your
nose into this case, are you?''

"Maybe.''

"Drop it, Kate.''

Now *I* was mad. Where did he get off ordering me
around? "It's a free country,'' I retorted.

The sheriff glared at me. "Kate McHaney, you're a stubborn woman."

The rest of the meal was shared in cold silence. I was still seething when I got back in my truck. Mingled with the anger was a crosscurrent of pain. Steve could do that to me. I wished I'd never met the rat. He had no business going around kissing me the way he had, getting me all involved, when he was still somehow hooked up with his wife from whom he had told me he was separated. He was a liar in addition to his other sins.

I sat there stewing for a while. Finally I managed to calm down. It took an effort to put a lid on my emotions. It helped to concentrate on the case. I reined in my thoughts about Steve and directed them toward Lorraine's murder and Freddie's involvement. I calmed down enough to give some objective thought to Steve's theory. Was it possible Freddie had strangled Lorraine? Could he have fooled me that much? It certainly was true that he had the most obvious motive.

I shook my head slowly, remembering his appearance and emotional state. If he was putting on an act, it was a good one. He'd have to be a better actor than a singer.

This started me thinking about Freddie Landers, and I realized I really didn't know him that well. I needed to get a better perspective on him, and I wanted to get some information about the members of the earlier band he had fronted. I ran through my mental list of people who knew Freddie and settled on his cousin Milton Bowman, who owned the recording studio that made the recording that propelled Freddie into stardom. Being related to Freddie, he would know as much about the singer-composer as anyone.

Cousin Milton's business was situated in the outskirts of one of the valley's larger communities, Greensborough, close to the border. It was a thirty-minute drive from Sheriff Gannon's bailiwick. I knew the area well and had no trouble finding Milt's Recording Studio.

The business was housed in a spacious one-story brick-and-masonry building. The grounds were landscaped with colorful tropical plants and royal palm trees. In the black-topped parking area was a white Cadillac bearing the individualized license plate *Milt*. It could belong only to Cousin Milton.

When I entered the building, I found myself in a reception area that had deep carpeting, indirect lighting, and soft, wired music. On the walls was some framed artwork that had been used on jackets of records produced by the studio. It appeared Cousin Milton was operating a very successful business. Behind a mahogany desk was Milton's well-fed wife, Elaine. She remembered me from the party on Freddie's ranch. Her Cupid's-bow lips smiled.

I asked to see her husband. The gold and silver bracelets on her plump arm jangled as she reached for the intercom. She spoke with Milton. Then she directed me down the hall to a door that led into Milton Bowman's private office.

It was a large room with probably the only large plate-glass windows in the building, not visible from the front. They gave a view of an enclosed patio area filled with lush plants and a bubbling fountain. Milton's office was paneled in mahogany and, like the reception area, deeply carpeted. The recording-studio owner came around a large desk piled high with papers and record-album covers to greet me. Again, as at the fiesta party on Freddie's ranch, he was decked out as if he were going somewhere to preach. Today he wore a suit of dark silk material, a monogrammed white shirt, black-and-white wing-tip shoes, and a maroon bow tie. He was out of uniform for the Rio Grande valley in August. The accepted style of attire in this semitropic climate in summer was open-collar sport shirts.

Milton Bowman was a cheerful, rotund individual with a pink, round face and shiny scalp. He had a warm smile and firm handshake. "Hello, Miss McHaney. Won't you have a seat?" He guided me into a chair of modern design.

"I wasn't sure if you'd remember me."

He sat on the corner of his desk, plump hands clasped in front of him, as he smiled at me. "Sure, I remember you. Freddie said you were a distant relative from Laredo, I believe."

"I'm afraid that's not exactly true."

He chuckled. "I suspected as much. I know about all our relatives. Family genealogy is a hobby of mine. I never heard of a relative in Laredo named Kate McHaney. Why was Freddie passing you off as a cousin?"

"I'm a private detective. Freddie wanted me to check on some things and thought it best to have me show up incognito."

"I see. And did you find what you were looking for?"

"Yes, as a matter of fact. But now I'm on a different assignment. Freddie has hired me to get to the bottom of his wife's murder."

Bowman's round face became solemn. The expression was incongruous. His round face was designed for perpetual affability. "What a terrible shock that has been. Poor Freddie."

"Yes, he's taking it pretty hard. How did you feel about Lorraine, Mr. Bowman?"

He looked surprised. "Me? Why, I'm not sure if I had any feeling about her one way or another. Since Freddie became a big-time star, I haven't seen much of him." He thought for a moment, then said slowly, "Lorraine was a beautiful woman, but I did get the impression that there was something of a hard, ambitious side to her nature. I thought she was more sophisticated and knowledgeable than Freddie. He's really kind of a naive fellow. She was a few years older than Freddie, I think. But he was head over heels in love with her, and that was what mattered. Do you have any leads on who might have killed her?"

"None at all at this point." I didn't see any reason to tell him that the sheriff's department considered Freddie high on the list of suspects. "I want to find out more about Freddie's life before he became famous. Did he grow up around here?"

"Yeah. He was orphaned at an early age. His parents were killed in a car wreck when Freddie was four or five. His mother was my mother's sister. He went to live with his uncle Roy Stovall, Freddie's father's brother. Uncle Stovall was a mean old warthog. I always felt sorry for Cousin Freddie. He lived out on that scraggly farm. Uncle Roy worked him hard and beat up on him when he got drunk, which was pretty regular. When Freddie was ten, Uncle Roy married a woman half his age and they had a child right off, Jeffrey. Poor Jeffrey is a sweet kid, but not completely right in the head—retarded, you know. The woman got fed up with the farm and Uncle Roy and taking care of a retarded child, and she split—ran off with some Yankee, a Midwest farmer winter tourist, and that was the last they saw of her. Freddie helped raise Jeffrey, and there's always been a close bond between them. Jeffrey's fifteen now, still living out on that miserable farm with his daddy. Uncle Roy is mean as ever, although I have to say he never mistreated Jeffrey the way he did Freddie, probably because the boy is his own.''

''That's quite a story,'' I said. ''How did Freddie get his musical training?''

''Oh, he just picked it up. Uncle Roy sure never sprang for any music lessons, you can bet on that. Freddie got ahold of an old guitar somewhere and fooled around with it, learning to pick out some chords. He had a natural ear and a God-given singing voice.'' Milton chuckled. ''That was the one thing I envied in Freddie. I've got a voice like a frog with laryngitis. Anyway, Freddie got some musicians together and started playing in beer joints up and down the border on Saturday nights. He made enough to get away from Uncle Roy. Then he married Tammie Sue—his first wife—and they moved into a ramshackle trailer home in Willow Springs. I think she's still living in the same place.''

It was easy to see that Cousin Milton was a terrible gossip and was going to be a great source of information.

''The musicians you mentioned that Freddie got together to play in the honky-tonks—were they his original band that made his first recording?''

''Yes. Billy Jo Turner, Addie Davis, Tommy Mason, Crawfish Willie Atkins, and Jimmy Joy Jamison. Tammie Sue sang with them. They were pretty fair weekend musicians. Nothing like the polished Nashville group that Freddie has backing him now, of course. To tell the truth, I never dreamed Freddie would amount to much. I figured he'd go on the rest of his life living in that run-down trailer house and playing for peanuts. Then one day he came around and asked me to make a record of a song he had written.

He didn't have the money to pay me, but I did it as a family favor. That was 'Remember Our Yesterdays.' As soon as I heard it, I thought the song had possibilities. I made some 45s and took them around to disc jockeys in the area. The song caught on right away and in no time was picked up by big-time deejays. Well, you know the rest. We all made some money out of that record, and it launched Freddie's career. Now he's a rich man and a national celebrity.''

"But all his other recordings were done by a big-time record company. Aren't you bitter about that?''

Milton laughed ruefully. "Oh, I razz Freddie about that some, but I have to be realistic. I don't have the promotional budget, distribution, and resources of those big companies. Freddie just outgrew me. We never had a formal contract, just a handshake. He had a perfect legal right to sign a contract with that Nashville recording company when they offered it to him. I say more power to him. The poor kid had a lousy childhood. He deserves some good times.''

I said, "I'd like to talk with those early band members. I understand three of them died recently.''

A shadow crossed his face. "That's what I heard. Billy Jo, Addie, and Tommy.'' He shook his head. "Sad. So many musicians die young. Booze, drugs, car wrecks, plane crashes. It can be a hard life. Two of the original band are still living: Crawfish Willie Atkins, the fiddle player, and Jimmy Joy Jamison, who plays saxophone.''

I took a notebook from my purse. "I wonder if you could tell me how to find these people, the musicians and Freddie's uncle. I'd like to talk to them.''

"Sure. Well, Uncle Roy has a little farm outside of San Benito. You take farm-to-market road 221 west of town. Go out about a mile and you'll see his name on the mailbox.

Now, the musicians, I'm not so sure. Last I heard, Jimmy Joy Jamison had a day job at a music store in McAllen. Crawfish Willie Atkins is another story. From what I've heard, Willie has been in and out of alcohol and drug rehabs the past few years. Jimmy Joy might know where he is."

"I'll find them." I thanked him for the information and the time he had given me. Before leaving, I asked him, "By the way, if you don't mind telling me, where were you that Friday morning when Lorraine was killed?"

His eyebrows shot up. "Me? Why, I was right here. Let me see, that was a Saturday morning. Yeah, we were recording a *conjunto* group, Los Alamos. We get a lot of business from the Hispanic community. Music is an important part of the Mexican culture, y'know."

I thanked him again and took my leave.

Chapter Nine

The mailbox bearing the name Roy Stovall was rusty and battered, like the dilapidated house that it served. I turned into the drive, rattled over cattle-guard pipes, and followed a short, rutted lane to the ramshackle farmhouse where Freddie Landers had lived as a child. It was pretty depressing. The weathered clapboard siding had long forgotten when it had its last coat of paint. The front porch sagged wearily. The tin roof was as rusty as the mailbox.

When I got out of the truck, a dog of indeterminate breed crawled from under the porch and barked halfheartedly. Then I heard music coming from the house. It sounded like an electric keyboard with multiple-instrument synthetic voicing.

I walked up the steps and across the porch to the front door, gingerly testing the rotting floorboards with each step. The rusty screen door suffered from numerous tears and patches. Through it, I could see into the front room of the house where a blond teenage boy was seated at the electronic keyboard. His long, thin fingers were flying over the keys like racing spiders.

I listened, entranced. When he ended the piece, I tapped on the door. He jumped up and peered at me through the screen.

"Hello," I said.

His large blue eyes stared at me.

"Are you Jeffrey?" I asked.

"Yeah. Who're you?"

"My name is Kate McHaney."

He continued to stare at me. "I don't know you."

"No, I don't believe you do, Jeffrey. That was a lovely piece you were playing. What was it?"

"I don't know. Somethin' I heard on the radio."

"You play beautifully."

He looked pleased.

"May I come in, Jeffrey?"

He became uncomfortable. "I don't know. Daddy said not to let strangers in."

"I'd like to hear you play some more."

"Well . . . okay."

He unlatched the screen door. I entered the room. It was obviously Jeffrey's room. There was a rumpled bed in one corner, and shirts and trousers hung on pegs on a wall. Everywhere I looked, I saw musical instruments—an electric guitar, a set of drums, several keyboards. They were all of first-class, expensive quality. They looked totally out of place in this shabby room.

"You have some beautiful instruments, Jeffrey."

"My brother, Freddie, gave me 'em," he said. He pointed to a large wall poster that bore Freddie Landers's picture. "That's my brother, Freddie," he said proudly.

"I know Freddie," I said. "We're friends. He's a real good musician. Can you play some more for me?"

"Sure." He picked up the guitar, struck a chord, then began a popular tune I'd been hearing recently. Halfway through, he either lost interest in the melody or forgot and strayed into something else that was unfamiliar to me. He seemed to wander from melody to melody, with bits and pieces, never completing a song. The musical expression flowed through him freely in all directions, like a river without direction or banks. As was the case with many mentally handicapped individuals, he had a natural artistic talent, but it was unschooled and unstructured.

He stopped after a while. I said, "That's pretty, Jeffrey. Do you read music?"

He shook his head. "Just hear something on the radio and play it, or make things up as I go along."

A door slammed somewhere in the back of the house. Then Roy Stovall appeared in the doorway. He was a scrawny individual dressed in a faded shirt, soiled blue jeans, and run-down boots. He had a leathery hide; small, suspicious eyes; and a scar down his left cheek, probably the result of a beer-joint brawl. I could smell sour beer, chewing tobacco, and unwashed body all the way across the room.

"Who th' heck are you?" he demanded. He swung his angry gaze to Jeffrey. I was surprised to hear his voice soften. "Son, ain't I told you a dozen times not to let strangers come in this house?"

The boy hung his head.

"That's all right, son. Try to remember next time. Now you go on back to the kitchen. I brung you some chocolate cake from town."

Jeffrey's face lighted up, and he scooted from the room. "The boy is retarded," Stovall explained. "Now, who are you and what are you doin' in my house? If you're one of them social workers pokin' your nose in my private business, then you're trespassin' and you're in big trouble, lady."

I did not think Roy Stovall would appreciate having a private detective on his premises any more than a social worker. It was safer to quickly shift professions. I opened my purse, shuffled through my assortment of business cards, and handed him the one that said I was a journalist with a national news syndicate. (I thought I'd have to get some more press cards printed if I kept up this act.)

"I'm writing an article about your famous nephew, Freddie Landers."

He scowled at the card. "What's that got to do with me?"

"Well, I understand you raised Freddie after his parents died. I'd like to learn all I can about his personal life. I thought you might be able to tell me something about his childhood."

Stovall shrugged. "Ain't much to tell. Freddie didn't amount to much, growin' up. He was lazy and dumb. Never could get him to do much work. He flunked out of school. Lucky he had that music talent. Made him a big shot—rich and famous."

"Jeffrey said Freddie gave him these musical instruments."

"Yeah, Freddie's always been good to Jeffrey. I'll give him that much. He gives the boy lots of things."

Something that had been tooling around in the back of my mind suddenly rang a bell. All the way out here, I had been trying to figure out how Roy Stovall might possibly figure in as a suspect in Lorraine's death. Now I could see a very strong motive.

"Freddie doesn't have any other close relatives, does he?" I asked.

"Reckon not. He was married to that fancy blond woman, but I heard she got herself killed. He's got some cousins, but he don't think much of them."

"But he's fond of Jeffrey."

"Oh, yeah. Like I said. He helped raise the boy. When they were youngsters, Freddie would beat up on the other kids if they made fun of Jeffrey. Jeffrey worships the ground Freddie walks on. Freddie wouldn't give me the time of day, but he does think the world of the boy."

"I guess Freddie has the boy in his will if anything happens to him."

"That's what he's told me."

Of course. That was it. A very good motive for Roy Stovall to want both Freddie and Lorraine dead. With Lorraine out of the way, there was a good chance that all of Freddie's estate would go to Jeffrey. As the boy's father and legal guardian, Roy Stovall would become rich too.

I asked a few more general questions, enough to make the interview sound convincing. I managed to find out that the Saturday when Lorraine was murdered, Roy Stovall had no alibi. He was here on the ranch, just him and Jeffrey.

Back in my pickup, driving out of the yard, I thought that I could definitely add Roy Stovall to the list of suspects. He might have made those attempts on Freddie's life, and he had reason enough to strangle Lorraine to remove the other possible heir and make Freddie look guilty by using Freddie's belt.

I ran into the usual brick wall, however, when I tried to fit Stovall into the deaths of Freddie's band members. It was the same frustration that had baffled me when I found out the truth about Lorraine. I could find ample reason for them to murder Freddie. But how did this tie in with the strange deaths of three other musicians? Or was there a connection?

By then it was midafternoon. I had time to make a couple more calls.

First I drove to the office of Sam Tompkins, the realtor who was involved in the Freddie Landers theme-park project. I didn't find out much more about him than I had learned at Freddie's party. No, he wasn't shedding any tears over Lorraine's demise. Good riddance as far as he was concerned. He didn't have a very good alibi for the time Lorraine was murdered, but that didn't appear to worry him.

From Tompkins, I did get the address of Kenneth Mayfield, Freddie's former business manager who had been fired by Lorraine. He, too, was high on my list of suspects.

I found Mayfield in a dinky one-room office on the third floor of a run-down office building in Harlingen. He was a middle-aged, painfully thin man, bald, hawk nosed, close-mouthed. He had a small accounting business. It was not flourishing.

There was no receptionist. When I opened the office door, I found myself looking at Mayfield, who was behind a desk piled high with papers. When I introduced myself as a private investigator, his normally dour visage became even more sullen. "I'm busy," he said shortly.

"This won't take long."

He didn't invite me to sit down.

"I understand you were Freddie Landers's business manager at one time."

"Who told you that?"

"Sam Tompkins."

He made no comment.

"Sam also said Freddie's wife fired you."

Still no comment. He just gave me a baleful stare.

"I don't suppose there was any love lost between you and Lorraine after that."

"She was a tramp," he said, an angry flush spreading over his sallow complexion. He clenched a sheet of paper into a ball and hurled it at a wastebasket.

"Why did she fire you?"

"She wanted complete control of Freddie's business affairs. She walked into my office one day, told me to pack up and get out. No notice, no severance pay. And me with a wife and a sick kid."

"I guess you weren't sorry to hear she'd been murdered."

"I didn't lose any sleep over it."

"Where were you that morning, the thirteenth, when she was killed?"

He stood up, shaking with rage. "All right, that does it. Get out of my office. You're not the police. I don't have to talk to you. You've got a lot of gall coming around here, making accusations."

Talk about hair-trigger temper. I thought *I* was hot-tempered. "Calm down," I said heatedly. "I'm not making accusations. Look, I'm just doing my job the way you are yours, and it's not a bed of roses being a single woman in the detective business. I've gotten dog-bitten trying to serve summonses, cussed out and threatened by guys who are ducking child-support payments, been paid with hot checks.

Just a week ago, somebody put knockout drops in my coffee, then tried to run me off the road and cause me to have a wreck. . . ."

I ran out of breath. We stared at each other. I must have touched a responsive chord. We were two poor clowns caught up in the struggle to keep our heads above water in a tough world. The look that passed between us signaled some kind of mutual kinship.

He sat down, looking tired and defeated. "All right. What else do you want to know?"

I took his change of manner as an invitation to have a seat, which I did in the nearest chair. "Not much. It might help to have some idea of Freddie's financial status. I'm wondering who would profit if he died."

Mayfield snorted. "Nobody, unless he hit a gold mine in the six months since his wife fired me. Freddie's broke. Not only broke, but everything he has is hocked up to the hilt, including his ranch and all his businesses."

That left me speechless. Freddie broke? That was surprising news. When I recovered, I asked, "But what happened to all his money?"

"I don't know." The accountant threw up his hands in a gesture of disgust. "Every month Freddie made regular, large cash withdrawals from his bank account. You can do that just so long before the well runs dry."

"What did he spend all that money on?"

"You tell me. I pleaded with him for some explanation. Maybe some of it could have been a tax write-off. Even certain gambling losses can be a legitimate deduction if that was what he was doing with it. But he refused to tell me anything."

I digested this surprising bit of information. I said slowly,

"It almost sounds as if he was paying somebody off. Do you think he was being blackmailed?"

"I have no idea, and it's no longer any concern of mine." This was a new development and, unfortunately, it added to Freddie's motive for killing Lorraine. If he was broke, he really needed that million-dollar life insurance. But why was he making those large monthly cash withdrawals? The word *blackmail* kept rattling around in my head.

After that little bombshell there wasn't much more Kenneth Mayfield could add.

I did ask him, "If Freddie is broke, how is he planning to finance his Freddie Landers theme park?"

"That's a big real-estate speculation balloon cooked up by Sam Tompkins and Lorraine. They're getting financing from investors. Freddie is strictly a guitar picker and singer. He doesn't have brains enough to handle a complicated land deal like that."

"With Lorraine out of the picture, what happens to it?"

"Sam Tompkins will go on handling it. He was the original promoter, anyway. He always did resent Lorraine sticking her greedy hands in it."

By the time I left Kenneth Mayfield's office, it was late afternoon. Riding around all day in August in a truck with a busted air conditioner had left me grimy, exhausted, and badly in need of a shower.

From Harlingen, I drove to Brownsville, arriving at sundown. I stopped at my office for a quick check on the mail and my telephone answering machine.

The phone machine light was on. I pressed the replay button. A flat, robotic voice with absolutely no inflection spoke in a monotone: "Kate McHaney, you are asking too many questions and poking your nose where it does not belong. Back off now, or some very bad things are going to happen to you.''

Then the room was acutely silent. The rays of the setting sun were streaking through the venetian blinds, creating golden, dust-flecked bars in the air. I looked at my scarred desk, at the green filing cabinet with my coffee maker on top, at my telephone, computer, fax machine, the wall calendar, and the couch against the wall.

Then my gaze swung back to the answering machine. I stared at it as if it were a snake about to strike.

The heat I'd suffered from all day was gone. I felt cold all over. I realized why the voice had sounded so mechanical. It had been generated on a computer. The fact that it was not human made the threat somehow even more chilling.

I locked up and went home. Romping with Bismark made me feel a little better. A shower made me feel a lot better.

I walked down to Catfish Charlie's place, enjoying the soft breeze and the lapping of the water. Sitting in my favorite booth in Catfish's place chased away some of the spooky feeling. Tonight was Benny Goodman night on Charlie's jukebox. The Goodman quartet was playing "Flying Home," one of Charlie's favorites.

Charlie came over, wiping his hands on his apron.

I said, "Hi, what's good?"

"Got some flounder just caught today. It's stuffed with crab meat and seasoning. With it, you get a salad, a baked potato, fresh string beans, and hush puppies."

"Okay, sounds good."

The truth was, I wasn't hungry. After hearing that emotionless robot voice threatening me, I had lost my appetite.

Charlie sat in the booth across from me. He looked at

me. "There was a guy in here this afternoon, asking questions about you. Wanted to know where you lived, where you worked, what time you got home. I gave him the brush-off, but I saw him talking to other people on the waterfront."

"Oh, yeah?" I moved the saltshaker in little circles. "Can you describe him?"

"Middle-aged guy. Chunky. Sandy hair. Looked tough, like a pro. Haven't seen him around here before. Oh, yeah, he had only one arm."

Chapter Ten

The one-armed man again—the guy who'd been there ahead of me when I had investigated Lorraine's background in Rio Dulce and again in Nashville. Now he was here and on my tail.

Charlie was giving me a searching look. "Kid, you look like you've seen a ghost. What kind of a case are you mixed up in, anyway?"

I didn't see a reason any longer for keeping the investigation confidential. It might make me feel better to talk about it, and I couldn't have picked a better audience. Charlie's eyes brightened, his leathery old face lighted up, and he leaned forward intently, listening to every word as I told him the whole story from the time Freddie first appeared in my office: my legwork in finding out about Lorraine's past, the attempt on my life, right up to the threat I'd heard on my answering machine this afternoon.

"Um-hmm. Sounds like you're getting close to some answers," Charlie observed, "if you've got them threatening you."

"Kind of seems that way."

There was an uneasy chill in the pit of my stomach. The person who'd left the message on my answering machine had murdered Lorraine. That same person might have killed three other times and wouldn't hesitate to kill again.

"Who do you pick for the killer?" Charlie asked.

I shrugged. "Almost everyone I've talked to has a good motive. Freddie's handicapped cousin, Jeffrey, would inherit his estate, so Uncle Roy Stovall would profit by Lorraine's and Freddie's deaths. Sam Tompkins, the realtor, wanted Lorraine out of the way. The business manager she fired, Kenneth Mayfield, hated Lorraine with a passion. Of course, there's Freddie himself. He had the best motive of all. Sheriff Gannon has about convinced himself Freddie did it. What has me beating my head against a brick wall is how Lorraine's deaths and the attempts on Freddie's life tie in with the deaths of the three musicians in Freddie's earlier band. I have the feeling there is a connection. What it is, though, I sure can't figure out."

"How about this one-armed guy?"

"Yeah, how does he fit into this crazy mess?"

Charlie leaned back, his lips pursed. "This reminds me of a case I worked on when I was with the FBI." He launched into an animated, lengthy narrative about one of his adventures, which, though highly entertaining, had absolutely no relationship to the case I was working on that I could see. But it did get my mind off my worries.

That night, I locked my door and slept with the loaded Winchester close to my bed.

I flat refused to drive around anymore in the August heat with a dead air conditioner. Early the next morning, I took the truck to a mechanic, Pancho Martinez, who ran a small repair shop in a tin shed a half mile down the beach from Catfish Charlie's.

Pancho fooled around under the hood with gauges, hoses, and cans of Freon for what seemed an interminable time, and finally gave me the bad news. "Needs a new compressor and evaporator."

"How much?"

He wiped his hands on a greasy red rag. "Parts and labor, five hundred bucks, give or take twenty."

I gave him a dirty look and lapsed into Spanish. I sometimes did that when I was disgusted. "Have you ever considered changing your name to Pancho Villa?" I weighed my anemic bank balance against another day of sticking to the vinyl upholstery in near hundred-degree heat. I sighed. "Okay, go ahead. When can I get it?"

"Tomorrow about this time."

I trudged back to the houseboat.

It seemed like a good time to take a break from the tension I'd been under. I was beginning to regret I'd ever gotten involved with this case. From now on, I resolved, I was going to stick to insurance investigations and missing persons.

Since I was taking the day off, I got out a fresh canvas and painting supplies and set them up on the deck of the houseboat. I tuned my portable radio to an FM station that played classical music. Then I set to work sketching a scene of a rusty barge making its way down the Intercoastal Canal. Clouds and sand dunes formed a backdrop for the setting, while sea gulls swooped over the barge.

For lunch, I made a chicken-salad sandwich. Wow, what a way to relax, sitting in the warm sunshine cooled by a breeze off the water, with a Franz Liszt concerto helping to sweep my brush over the canvas. I could almost forget my life had been threatened.

Late that afternoon, Bismark, who was curled on the deck beside me, raised his head and let out a throaty woof. I turned to see a Ford Bronco parking at the dock where the houseboat was tied up. A man and a boy got out. My brush gave a jerk, making a smear. The man was Steve Gannon. The five-year-old boy with him had to be his son. The kid had the same wavy brown hair, the same gray eyes framed with beautiful long lashes.

Steve was not wearing his usual sharply creased sheriff's uniform. He was dressed casually in a sport shirt and blue jeans. I found myself incredibly glad to see him.

He came up on deck, holding the boy's hand. "Hi," he said somewhat awkwardly.

Bismark trotted up to the boy, sniffing his pants leg and wagging his tail.

"Hello," I replied, also self-conscious.

"This is my boy, Mark. Son, say hello to Miss Mc-Haney."

"Hello," the boy said gravely. "What's your dog's name?"

"Hello, Mark." I wiped paint-smeared fingers on a turpentine rag and shook hands with the boy. "The dog is Bismark. You can pet him. He won't bite. He loves kids."

Mark gave Bismark a pat, and the dog rolled over, wriggling in ecstasy. Instant friendship.

"You said I could bring him out sometime to fish off the deck of your houseboat," Steve reminded me.

"Sure. Glad to have you." That was an understatement.

"We brought fishing gear and bait. Don't let us disturb your painting."

"That's okay. I've been at it all day. I'm about painted out."

"Can I have a look?"

"Well, don't expect much," I said, suddenly overcome with uncharacteristic shyness. "I'm no Rembrandt."

"I'm no art critic." He moved around to look at my canvas. He studied the painting thoughtfully. "You know, that's really good. I'm very impressed. I had no idea you were an artist."

"I'm not," I said, feeling flustered as I cleaned my brushes and packed away my tools. "It's just a hobby, a way to relax. My car's in the shop, so I'm taking the day off."

"I have the afternoon off too. I've been promising to take Mark fishing. I'd told him about your houseboat, so we decided to drive out on the chance you might be home."

"Well, Mark," I said, "let's get your fishing pole and see if they're biting today."

I got my rod and reel and we all had a great time, fishing until sundown. We caught several croakers and one nice redfish.

After it got dark, Steve cleaned the fish. I made a salad and warmed up some rolls and then broiled the fish. While I prepared the meal, Steve and Mark took turns sitting in my barber's chair. Mark thought it was real neat. Over supper, Steve and I had a glass of wine while Mark had a soft drink. Very domestic scene.

Later, we sat out on the deck on lawn chairs. It was a soft, luminous summer night. A full moon spread a golden path over the water. Small waves lapped softly against the hull, giving a gentle rocking motion. Lights from barges moved down the Intercoastal Canal and melted in the distance.

Mark played with Bismark for a while, riding him like a pony. Finally, he got tired and went to sleep, curled up in his father's lap.

There was silence for a while, just the splash of the water and the distant rumble of a tug's diesel. I felt tension crackling in the air again the way it did the night Steve kissed me. He was deep in thought. The big, silent Texan was wrestling with words. *Who needs him?* I thought. *Let him stew in his own juice.* I wasn't going to help him this time.

Finally, he said, "Kate, I haven't had my head on straight since I kissed you. I—I hadn't planned on anything like this happening. . . ." His voice trailed off.

He was doing a lousy job of this.

I waited.

I looked over the water to a star separated from the others in the velvet sky. It looked lonely, the way I felt. I always did have lousy luck with men, I thought.

"What you're trying to tell me is that you're not as separated from your wife as you first said."

"No. I don't know why I said 'separated.' I guess it was a kind of defense I automatically put up to avoid any kind of emotional entanglement. Actually, we're divorced—have been for a year. It was a very unhappy marriage . . . bad for both of us. Elaine left me several times. When Mark was born it was the last straw. She's a very ambitious woman. She's working for a law degree. When she asked for a divorce, she wanted me to have custody of Mark. She said she was not cut out to be a mother.

"As you can imagine, this unhappy marriage and divorce left me emotionally shell-shocked," Steve said. "Also, pretty bitter. I didn't want to have anything to do with falling in love again. I'd made up my mind I was never going to remarry. Then you came along and got me totally confused. I don't like the feelings that have been boiling up in me for you, Kate. And it isn't fair to you, getting mixed up with a guy as emotionally banged up as I am.''

''Maybe,'' I said unsteadily, ''I'm willing to take my chances.''

He looked at me gravely. ''You're a pretty special person, you know that, K. R. McHaney? I wish I'd met you a long time ago, long before I ever saw Elaine. But I didn't. I think it's better for both of us if we cool it for now. Let me try to get my head on straight.''

I thought Elaine must be a colossal dope to leave a man like Steve Gannon and a terrific kid like Mark. Guess it takes all kinds to make the world.

From the tortured look on Steve's face, I thought she must have led him a dog's life. Strange, what some men will put up with. I could see why he didn't want to get involved again.

What the heck. I didn't really want a man in my life. I loved my freedom. Then I looked at his handsome profile outlined against the sky and thought, *Who am I kidding?* But I shrugged. ''It's no big deal, Steve. Don't lose any sleep over it.''

''I am losing a lot of sleep,'' he said. ''I don't want to lose you, Kate.''

''I'm not going anywhere. I'll be around. If you get things straightened out in your mind, drop on by sometime.''

We left it at that. Steve kissed me good night, making my knees go weak again, much to my chagrin. Then he carried his sleeping son to his car.

I watched the taillights of the Bronco disappear down the beach. Bismark sensed the lonely void inside me and put his face on my knees, giving a soft whimper.

Sometimes I got homesick to see my family. Here I was at the southern tip of Texas without a relative within two thousand miles. As much as I valued my independence, there were times when I felt all alone in the world. I thought as soon as I could save up enough money, I was going to take a trip back to New York.

I went to bed, again propping the Winchester beside me. Bismark curled up on the floor near the bed.

I fell into a sleep filled with grotesque dreams. I dreamed I was sinking in quicksand. Steve had his hand stretched out to me, but he couldn't reach me. Then I was in a place that was very warm. I thought it must be hell, because hot, flickering lights were all around me. Bismark was barking at me.

I came groggily awake and realized that Bismark *was* barking and tugging at the sheet. There *were* flickering lights all around, and it was very hot.

I saw it then, the orange flames flaring up outside all the windows. With a cry, I leaped out of bed. I ran around and saw the same thing out of every window. The entire deck of the houseboat was ablaze. I smelled burning wood and tar. I began coughing as smoke filled the room.

I knew I had less than a minute to get out of there before I was overcome with smoke. But I was trapped.

Chapter Eleven

If I opened the door, the flames would burst into the room. Anyway, there was no place I could go if I got through the door. The entire deck was a raging inferno.

In the kitchen alcove, there was a small stairway going up to the roof of the cabin. I sometimes used it when I wanted to sit on the roof. You got a better view up there than from the deck. I stumbled to the stairway. My eyes were streaming and I was coughing violently. Bismark was whimpering. I grabbed his collar, made him go with me to the roof. Up there, I was able to breathe a little better, but my situation was desperate. The cabin was on fire now. In minutes, the roof was going to collapse under me, plunging us into the raging furnace below.

I heard a fire siren and saw headlights of the volunteer fire department truck barreling down the beach toward us, but they couldn't get here in time to help me.

"Bismark, we have to jump," I yelled above the crackling, rushing sound of the fire.

The dog was confused, at a loss to know what to do except to crouch against my leg and whimper.

The deck below, along the side of the cabin, was narrower than the fore and aft section. Desperation and panic gave me a surge of adrenaline. I picked up the big dog and heaved him overboard. He went sailing through the air, twisting, legs threshing; he just cleared the deck and hit the water with a splash.

The flames were higher now, obscuring my view of the edge of the deck. If I jumped, I'd have to go right through the red-orange blaze. My throat was on fire. With every gasping breath, I dragged more smoke into my tortured lungs. There was a smothering weight on my chest. My choice was to jump now or stand here and die.

I gathered what strength was left in my legs and jumped blindly through a wall of leaping flames. I thought I would probably hit the edge of the deck and turn into a cinder. Instead, I felt the welcome smack of my body hitting water. I went down into the cool, green depths. Struggling weakly, I got back to the surface and floundered my way to the beach.

By then the fire truck had arrived and the volunteer firemen were scurrying around, getting their pump going and sending streams of water over the burning hull.

It was too late. The cabin was already gone. The hull was a mass of smoking, hissing timbers burned almost down to the waterline.

I sat there, glumly staring at what had been my home the past two years. All my personal possessions were gone— my clothes, books, records, dishes, painting supplies and finished canvasses, the fine Winchester rifle, my purse with all my credit cards, the barber chair. . . .

When I thought about the barber chair was when I came closest to crying. I loved that chair. Where would I ever find another? I felt so alone at that moment, and I suddenly thought of Steve. How I wished he were here! But he had just given me that big speech about needing some space, and the last thing I wanted was for him to feel sorry for me. I'd have to handle this on my own.

All I had left of my clothes was the shortie pajamas I was wearing. A fireman had given me a blanket to put around myself. He had also brought a container of oxygen to counteract the smoke in my lungs.

Several cars had pulled up beside the fire truck. One of them was a rusty beach buggy. It belonged to my landlord. Catfish Charlie clambered stiffly from behind the wheel and came over to sit beside me. His wavy mop of white hair was tousled. His clothes looked as if he'd jumped out of bed and grabbed the nearest thing handy. He was wearing bedroom slippers.

I removed the oxygen mask. "Charlie, I'm so sorry. Your houseboat—"

"Listen, kid, don't worry about that," he said gruffly. "I want to know if you're all right. Did you get burned?"

"Just singed. I don't think I have any eyebrows left."

"You want me to take you to the hospital?"

I shook my head. The only thing that was keeping me from crying was that I was so mad. "Charlie, that fire was no accident. Someone is trying to kill me—the same one who has been stalking Freddie Landers's band, killing the musicians one by one, who murdered Lorraine, and who put that warning message on my answering machine."

"Sure looks like it," he agreed.

"He's got me mad now. I'm going to get him."

"If he doesn't get you first. Don't you think maybe you'd better back off from this case, Kate?"

"No! It's too late, anyway. He won't stop now. He has to shut me up. Somehow in my poking around, I've gotten too close to the answer. I have to figure it out to save my own hide now. Charlie, it's my fault you've lost your houseboat." The tears were back, stinging my eyes.

"I told you not to worry about that. I had it insured. I'll find a hull somewhere and build you another houseboat. In the meantime, you can stay with me. I've got a little garage efficiency behind my house. It's not much bigger than a closet, but it has indoor plumbing and it's clean."

I got a lump in my throat. Charlie and I had become sort of family. He was as close to a father as I'd ever had.

In a choked voice, I said, "You're a good man, Charlie Brown." It was a dumb thing to say, but Charlie understood. He patted my hand. Then he helped me up, and I walked, wrapped up in the blanket, to his beach buggy. Bismark trotted along beside me.

Charlie lived in a modest frame house on the beach a short distance from his restaurant. I never could decide how well-off he was financially. Judging from the beachcomber clothes he wore and the rusty beach buggy he drove, he was barely getting by. But I knew for a fact that he owned rental property, small one-family houses, all over the area.

When we got to his house, Charlie scrounged up a shirt and trousers for me to wear. It was from his wardrobe of beachcomber attire and had frayed cuffs and numerous patches, but it had been freshly laundered.

His description of the efficiency apartment above his garage was accurate. I'd seen walk-in closets that were bigger.

But it had a bathroom and a bed. The bed was essential. I was in a state of nervous exhaustion. I collapsed into the bed. Bismark curled up on the floor beside me. In no time we were both asleep.

The next morning, I borrowed Charlie's beach buggy. I left Bismark with Charlie and drove over to check on my truck. Pancho Martinez told me it would be noon before he finished working on it, so I drove into town in Charlie's rattletrap car.

First, I had to hire a locksmith to unlock my office door and make a new set of keys, the old ones having been lost in the fire with my purse. I spent a good part of the morning on the phone calling for replacement credit cards. Then I drove to the highway Department of Safety to apply for a new driver's license. I elicited a lot of curious looks. No wonder, in the getup I was wearing—ragged shirt and baggy trousers several sizes too big and a pair of floppy tennis shoes that fit Charlie but missed my size in footwear by several numbers. Add to that my missing eyebrows, and I must have looked like somebody who had slept in a Dumpster the night before.

My next stop was a clothing store, where I purchased a supply of underwear, blue jeans, shirts, shoes, and a pair of boots and jogging shoes. Fortunately, I'd had an extra checkbook in my office safe.

I had a hamburger, then spent an hour at Kim Song's Karate studio, working out some of my pent-up anger, fright, and frustration.

By then I'd given Pancho Martinez plenty of time to finish working on my truck. I stopped at Catfish Charlie's to take him with me to drive his beach car back and we went to Pancho's repair shed. True to his promise, the truck was ready. It hurt to write out the check for five hundred dollars, but I felt better about it when I got in the truck and cool air-conditioning washed over me.

In comfort, I drove first to Freddie Landers's ranch. I had some questions to ask that gentleman about his curious financial status. Freddie wasn't there. The maid told me he was off somewhere on the border with the filming company. At least that gave him an alibi for the time someone set the houseboat afire last night.

Or did it? Could he have driven from the filming location in his fast sports car the way Steve theorized he had done the day Lorraine was murdered?

Possibly, but I had trouble casting Freddie in the role of a murderer and arsonist. He had been too genuinely frightened when he first told me about the killer stalking his band, and too sincerely broken up over Lorraine's death.

Next on my list were the two surviving members of Freddie's band. Maybe they could give me the missing link between the deaths of the three band members, the attempts on Freddie's life, and the murder of Lorraine.

It gave me a shaky feeling, driving around knowing that now I was being stalked the same as the musicians who had died. The killer had missed getting me in the fire, but he wasn't going to give up. I had become too dangerous to him. I found myself glancing apprehensively at the rearview mirror, nervous about any car that stayed behind me too long. I didn't feel nearly as brave now as I had right after the fire. I felt as if I were sitting on a ticking time bomb and the only thing that was going to save me was to find some answers fast. Since yesterday, the case had taken on a whole new dimension. I wasn't only working for a client, now; I was trying to save my own hide.

My first stop was McAllen. There were several music stores in the town. After asking a few questions, I found the store where Jimmy Joy Jamison worked.

Jimmy was about Freddie's age, mid-twenties. He had a bland, smooth face, pale eyes, and blond hair. When I walked into the store, he was behind a counter, chatting with a customer. I waited until the customer left; then I approached Jimmy Joy. I gave him my card, the right one this time. He looked at it and his eyes narrowed. "Lady private detective, huh. What can I do for you?" His voice was cool, his expression cautious.

"Freddie Landers has asked me to check into some things for him. You know Freddie, of course."

He shrugged noncommittally.

"I understand you played in his band at one time."

There was a guarded look in his eyes. "Maybe. I've played in a lot of bands."

I could see already I was not going to get much out of this character.

"Maybe you remember being with him when he recorded his first hit, 'Remember Our Yesterdays.' "

"I don't remember."

"Your name is on the album cover as one of the sidemen."

"Then I guess I was there."

"I don't see how you could forget. That was big news in the music business in this area. The record made a lot of money. You must have gotten your share."

He didn't respond, just looked at me with a blank expression.

He was beginning to irk me. "I bet you make a great poker player," I said.

"What's that supposed to mean?"

"Never mind. How did you feel after Freddie hit the big time, left you guys behind, and replaced you with some hotshots out of Nashville?"

"How was I supposed to feel?"

"Bitter. Mad. Resentful. It would be the natural reaction."

"I'm not into bitter and mad, lady. It makes bad vibes."

I felt as if I were banging my head against a brick wall.

"What did you think of Freddie's second wife, Lorraine?"

"Never met the lady."

"Did you know she'd been murdered?"

"I think I read something about that in the paper."

"Ever see Freddie since you played in his band?"

"Nope."

I wasn't getting the response I had expected. If he was scared out of his wits the way Freddie's first wife, Tammie Sue, was, he was doing a good job of covering it up. The same for any animosity he might feel toward Freddie Landers. Tammie Sue had said the members of Freddie's first band hated Freddie's guts. If that was the case with Jimmy Joy, he sure wasn't telling anyone about it.

I tried another tack. "I've heard that several of the other guys from the band died recently."

He frowned. A shadow crossed his face, the first reaction I'd gotten out of him.

I asked, "You think those guys might have been murdered?"

He paled visibly. Aha! I'd finally found a crack in his defense mechanism. His voice was shaky. "That's heavy stuff, lady. The police said they were all accidents. Billy Joe got run over. Addie was knifed by a mugger. Tommy got drunk, went to bed with a cigarette, and burned himself up.''

"Yes, that's what the police said. Seems coincidental, though. Three in a row like that, all within a few months. Then Freddie's wife gets murdered.''

Jimmy Joy shrugged, drawing back in his shell. "I don't know anything about stuff like that.''

"That leaves just two—you and Crawfish Willie Atkins. You're the only sidemen from Freddie's first band who haven't met with violent deaths.''

He said nothing. He was all walled up again in his private fortress.

He was being no help whatsoever. I decided I'd better give up before I hit him with a bassoon that was lying on the counter.

Maybe I'd have better luck with the other surviving band member. "Have any idea where I could find Crawfish Atkins?'' I asked.

The saxophone player muttered, "That's a sad case. Poor Willie. Too many drugs, too much liquor. Last I heard, he'd just gotten out of the hospital for about the fifth time. He's in Brownsville, I think. I don't know his address. His brother lives down there. He might know. His name is Jack W. Atkins. He's probably listed in the phone book.''

"Well, thanks. I'll see if I can locate him.''

"Yeah, well, tell him I said hi.''

From McAllen, I took the Interstate down to Brownsville. As I drove, I pondered my meeting with Jimmy Joy Jamison. Had he clammed up because he was involved in this situation? Or was it because he was scared of what would happen to him if he talked?

I got off at the business exit. This took me downtown,

where I stopped at my office and consulted my phone book. I found the listing for J. W. Atkins, jotted down the address, then drove to that part of town.

It was a poor section of small, ramshackle houses. In this hot, arid climate, lawns were luxuries requiring constant watering. In the poverty ghettos like this, the frame and adobe houses crouched close together, fences had gaps in the boards like broken teeth, and front yards were bald patches of bare, sun-baked dirt. The only vegetation that survived were native thorny trees such as huisache or mesquite and some clumps of cactus.

I found the number of the Atkins residence, parked my truck at the curb of the narrow street, and walked up to the front steps. When I knocked, the door was opened by a plump housewife holding a fat baby on one hip. The late afternoon heat had made her face shiny and left damp half moons under the arms of her shapeless, faded house dress. "Yeah?"

"Hello. I'm looking for Willie Atkins. Do you know him?"

"Yeah, he's my brother-in-law."

"I'd like to talk to him."

She didn't appear suspicious or question my motives. In my blue jeans and white shirt, which was suffering the ravages of the dust and heat of August, I probably fit right into the neighborhood.

She pushed a strand of blond hair from her perspiring forehead. Her baby started fretting. She worked a little body English to give him a bouncing motion. "If it's about a music job, Willie ain't up to playing right now. He's been sick."

"No, it's not about music."

"Well, he don't live here. He's got an apartment a few streets over. He just moved there. Wait a minute, I'll get you the address."

She left and came back in a few moments with an address scribbled on a piece of paper.

I thanked her and drove to the address. It was a garage apartment in the same economically depressed neighborhood. I knocked on the door, but there was no answer. The shades were drawn, and I heard no sounds inside.

I went back to the truck. Then I noticed a saloon on the corner at the end of the block.

The Stardust Lounge was a beer joint that did not live up to its glamorous name. It was a square-frame, flat-roofed building sitting on a corner lot otherwise occupied with weeds, tin cans, and the rusting carcasses of two wrecked cars. The shuttered windows were protected with black wrought-iron burglar bars. The faded sign bearing the bar's name included the drawing of a shooting star and looked as if it had been painted by a half-drunk customer.

On a hunch, I locked the truck and walked down to the lounge. It was one of those neighborhood bars where fat women with curlers in their hair sat around in the afternoon, smoking, drinking beer, and gossiping while men stood at the bar or played pool on the two tables in the alcove off the main room.

I stood just inside the doorway while my vision adjusted to the darkness after the glare outside.

The jukebox was blaring a Willie Nelson song. The late-afternoon beer drinkers were settling in at tables and booths. I checked them out. It was a blue-collar crowd. Some were from road crews, with white caliche dust in their hair, others were construction workers, still wearing their hard hats.

I spotted a lone beer drinker who looked as if he might be a country-western musician fresh out of a rehab center. I based my guess on his wide-brimmed Western hat. His shirt, jeans, and boots looked as if they had come from a closeout sale at Goodwill. He had long, dirty brown hair tied in a ponytail, a drooping mustache, and one earring. If that wasn't Crawfish Willie Atkins, it should be.

I slid into the booth on the seat facing him. "Willie Atkins?" I asked.

He gave me a startled, frightened look. "Yeah . . . who're you?"

"Kate McHaney. Private investigator." I laid my business card in front of him.

He had a bad case of the shakes. He was just barely able to get his glass of beer to his lips without spilling it down his shirtfront.

"I'm doing some investigating for an old friend of yours, Freddie Landers."

"Yeah?" He gave me a wary look.

"I'd like to ask you some questions about the days when you played in Freddie's band."

A film of perspiration appeared on his forehead. "What kind of questions?"

"Well, three of the musicians who played in that band have died under strange circumstances this past year. I talked with Freddie's ex-wife, Tammie Sue. She's pretty badly frightened. She thinks somebody is out to get all of you. Now Freddie's second wife, Lorraine, has been murdered. I want to know if you can tell me anything that happened when you were with Freddie's band that could explain why someone's after you people."

Atkins took out a handkerchief and patted the cold sweat on his forehead. "Why should I talk to you about that?"

"Very simple. It could save your life. If there's a reason somebody is out killing off you guys, you should see he's put in jail before he gets around to you. I tried to talk to Jimmy Joy, but he wouldn't give me the time of day. I'm hoping you have better sense."

A bitter smile twisted Atkins's lips. "Maybe Jimmy's the one with better sense."

He shook a cigarette from a crumpled pack and lit it with shaking hands. It was obvious he was a chain-smoker. His index and middle fingers were stained yellow from tobacco tar.

I tried a different approach. "When Freddie got famous, he dumped you. Tammie Sue thinks you guys hate his guts."

Atkins snorted. "Don't believe anything Tammie Sue tells you. She's a lush. She's the one who hates Freddie, because he got tired of her boozing, dumped her, and married Lorraine. Freddie's a good guy. He's picked up the tab on my hospital bills."

"Why would he do that?"

"Because that's the kind of guy Freddie is. He don't forget his friends. He's good-hearted. He couldn't help dumping us. You get in with those big-time recording companies and bookers and you do what they tell you or one day an ugly guy in a pin-striped suit comes around and breaks your arm. Freddie Landers became big business. He's just a simpleminded, good-hearted country boy. I don't think he quite knows how to handle it."

I was pleased that Atkins was loosening up. I had the feeling he knew something, and if I could gain his confidence, he might tell me. I bought him another round of beer.

As the beer mellowed him out, I got him to talking about the days he was with Freddie's band, when they were barnstorming up and down the border, playing anywhere they could get a one-night stand.

"Tell me about the song Freddie wrote that brought him all this fame."

He had sucked his cigarette down to a stub. He lit another off the smoldering tip. He coughed a couple of times and drank some beer. "Well, he showed up with it on the bandstand one night. He'd written some other tunes before, but they were just run-of-the-mill stuff. This one, 'Remember Our Yesterdays,' was different. It was good. I knew that the first time we played it. We started using it, and wherever we played it, people liked it. They'd request it, and they'd ask if it was on a record. That gave Freddie the notion for us to record the tune. It costs money to put out a record album, and in those days Freddie was broke all the time, same as the rest of us. He finally got some backing from Sam Tompkins."

That stunned me. When I recovered from the surprise, I asked, "Sam Tompkins the realtor?"

"Yeah."

"You're telling me Freddie knew Sam Tompkins that far back? I thought they just got acquainted when they started the Freddie Landers theme-park project."

Atkins shook his head. "Tompkins loves country-western music. He liked our band, used to hire us when he gave parties for real-estate buyers. When Freddie told him about the record he wanted to make, Sam agreed to advance him the financing."

"But Freddie's cousin Milton told me he did the recording for Freddie as a favor."

Atkins grinned, revealing yellowed teeth with some gaps. "Cousin Milton? That's a laugh. Milton Bowman is as tight as they come. He wouldn't even give Freddie a break on the price of doing the recording. He cut the master in his studio and sent it off to some outfit in Japan that stamps the records. I think the artwork and covers were done in Houston. Milton did a good job on recording the master, I'll say that. And the covers looked nice, real professional. I think they made only about a thousand copies to start with. Of course, when it caught on like it did, they put out a bunch more."

"I guess Freddie cut some kind of deal with Sam Tompkins to give him a share of the profits in exchange for the original financing," I surmised.

"Oh, you can be sure of that. Sam is very sharp when it comes to making deals. Freddie is no businessman. He signed away most of the profits from 'Remember Our Yesterdays.' Sam Tompkins was the one who made the big bucks off that one. Milton was kicking himself for not doing the recording for Freddie on some kind of royalty-percentage deal. As it was, all he got out of it was his cost for making the records. The rest of us got even less, just peanuts. Sam is still getting royalties off the sales of 'Remember Our Yesterdays.' Freddie didn't start getting rich until he went with the Nashville recording studio and played those concert tours."

This information was very enlightening. It added a whole new dimension to the involvement of Sam Tompkins in Freddie's affairs.

"Mr. Atkins," I said, "you've been in on all this from

the beginning. You must have some idea of who wants you band members out of the way, even to the point of resorting to murder.''

Atkins seemed on the verge of saying something, but at that point, he glanced over my shoulder, toward the front entrance, and his complexion turned the color of dishwater. ''I've got to go,'' he said, getting up so fast he tipped his glass over, splashing beer across the table.

I jumped up too, quickly dug some money out of my purse to pay for the beer, and dropped it on the table.

Catfish Atkins was already out the front door. I don't know when I've seen anyone move so fast. I got to the door behind him. By then it was pitch dark outside. I heard tires screech and saw taillights vanishing down the street. Atkins had taken off running in the opposite direction, toward his apartment. I was amazed that anyone just out of the hospital could run so fast.

I followed him, but by the time I got to the garage apartment, he was inside and had locked the door. I pleaded with him to let me in, but he just told me to go away. Finally I shoved another one of my business cards under the door and asked him to contact me when he felt like talking some more.

I suddenly became aware of how black the night was. There were no streetlights. The neighborhood was silent, deserted. There wasn't another living soul around. I thought about that car that had driven away from the bar so fast. What if it were still cruising around the neighborhood and would circle back here any minute? Small hairs on the back of my neck prickled. I suddenly wanted, in the worst way, to get back in my truck and lock the doors.

Chapter Twelve

I am no hero. I do not like this business of running scared. Right now, I was wishing I'd gone into an entirely different line of work. At least before I got involved in the Freddie Landers mess, the cases I handled did not have fatal overtones. A few times I'd been chased by dogs sicced on me by someone on whom I was trying to serve court orders, or threatened bodily harm by creeps who wouldn't pay their child support, but I hadn't had a psychopathic killer stalking me.

I didn't breathe easy until an hour later when I was in Catfish Charlie's place, safely surrounded by waterfront characters, the smell of fish and beer, the rattle of dishes, and Fats Waller singing "I Love You, But Your Feet's Too Big" on Charlie's jukebox.

It was a busy night for Charlie, but that didn't keep him from spending some time at my table discussing the case. I told him about the surprising development of Sam Tompkins's being involved in the recording deal of Freddie's first record. I also told him about the theory that was beginning to take shape in my mind. "Charlie, I've become convinced that that first record of Freddie's, 'Remember our Yester- days,' is where this whole thing ties together. Almost all the people I've talked to—Freddie's first wife, the musicians who are still living, Sam Tompkins, Freddie himself— they're all involved in that recording. Tomorrow I'm going to have a soulful talk with Freddie Landers. I think that gentleman has been holding out on me."

Charlie looked worried. "I'm uneasy about your running around all over the place with a killer dogging your heels. Don't you think you'd be smart to bring the cops in on this?"

"I sure plan to, just as soon as I have something I can show them. So far, I'm going on hunches and speculation."

"You know, speaking of cops, that sheriff came by this morning. He nearly had a fit when he found out about the fire—wanted to know why you didn't call him. He said he'd been going crazy trying to find you."

"I don't know why," I said. "There wasn't anything he could have done." Secretly I was pleased that Steve had been so worried, but there was no need to tell Catfish that.

"Well, anyway, he almost didn't believe me when I said you were out. He's called three more times today. What's going on with you two?"

"Not a thing, Catfish, not a thing."

"You'd make things a lot easier on yourself if you'd tell him what's going on."

The look in my eyes must have told him that I had no intention of doing that.

"Well, I know you're going to do things your way, no matter what I say. You lost your rifle in the fire. I left something in your room that can give you some protection."

I found that "something" on my bed when I returned to the garage apartment. It was a 12-gauge double-barreled shotgun, the kind the old Western guys used when they rode shotgun on stagecoaches. It had short barrels and old-fashioned, exposed hammers on each side. Beside it was a box of buckshot shells.

I had no idea where Charlie got the thing. It was not exactly a lady's weapon. A blast from that blunderbuss would blow out a wall and kick me into the next room. I felt the mixed urge to giggle and to cry at Charlie's rather clumsy attempt to provide me with some protection. I was touched by his concern at a time when everyone else seemed out to get me. I had to admit a gun like that would tend to discourage an arsonist. I slept a little better with the little cannon propped beside my bed.

The next day, I hung it in my truck in the rack in plain view across the rearview mirror and stuffed the box of shells under the seat. Then I tried to call Steve just to tell him I was okay, but I couldn't reach him. Probably just as well, I decided.

When I drove out to Freddie's ranch, I was told that he was still on location with the movie company, so I drove down to the border village where they were filming *The Freddie Landers Story*. It was the real story I was after, and I told Freddie so in no uncertain terms when I found him in his private trailer that had been provided by the movie company.

Freddie was dressed in the kind of getup he wore when fronting his band—boots, jeans, fringed jacket, wide-brimmed hat. He was sitting in front of a dressing-table mirror, drinking coffee and puffing one of his long, skinny cheroots. There were several other people in the trailer—a technician touching up his makeup for a scene they were preparing to shoot, some other film-crew types, and Freddie's omnipresent bodyguard, a big guy with an ugly scar down the side of his face who looked like the villain in a grade-B Western. He even wore a black hat.

I got right to the point. "Freddie, I need to talk to you alone for a few minutes."

He looked annoyed. "Well, heck, Miss McHaney, I got to be on the set in a little while. Can't it wait?"

"No, it can't. There have been some developments in this case I have to talk to you about. It involves personal matters that I don't think you want me to broadcast in public."

That got his attention. His look of annoyance changed to an expression of uneasiness. He asked the others to leave us alone for a few minutes. His bodyguard was giving me a sour look and grudgingly left only when Freddie insisted.

"Want some coffee?" he asked.

"Yeah, thanks, I could use it. I didn't have time for breakfast."

He removed a towel stained with flesh-colored makeup from around his neck and filled a cup from a coffee maker on the dressing-room table. He handed it to me, then went over, flopped in an easy chair, and crossed his boots on a handy coffee table. He was trying to look casual, but my powers of observation told me he was uptight and wary.

The coffee was rich and good. I enjoyed a few sips, then put the cup in the saucer. I was seething inwardly, and the words came pouring out. "Freddie, a lot has been going on since you told me to keep working on this case. I've gotten threatening phone calls. I was almost killed when my houseboat was set on fire by an arsonist."

He turned pale. "Why, that's awful, Miss McHaney. I don't know what to say. I didn't know you'd be in any danger—"

"Didn't you, Freddie?" I demanded, looking at him hard and searchingly. "I think you know a lot more than you've told me."

He began getting a cornered look. He moistened his lips. "I don't know what you're talkin' about." He got up and began moving restlessly around the room. "Now, look, I don't know what this is all about, but I guess I made a mistake hiring you to keep checking into Lorraine's death. I was real bad shook up after the funeral, and I guess I wasn't thinkin' straight. I should have left stuff like that up to the police. Anyway, why don't you just drop this now. You figure out what I owe you so far—"

Wait a minute. I thought. *This is getting curiouser and curiouser.* It did, however, add credence to the theory that had been taking shape in my mind.

"You're suddenly singing a different tune, Freddie. When you first came to me, you were scared out of your wits that somebody was out to get you. Aren't you worried about that anymore?"

He waved his hand holding the cigar. "You pretty well solved that when you found out about Lorraine's background. At first, I didn't want to believe that Lorraine made those attempts to kill me, but since the funeral I've had time to think about it and I've made myself face the facts. It must have been Lorraine tryin' to do me in, the way she probably did to them first two husbands to collect the life insurance. Now that she's gone, there ain't been no more attempts on my life. So, if you'll figure out how much I owe you—"

"What are you going to pay me with, Freddie? Unless, of course, you collect the million-dollar life insurance on Lorraine. Other than that, you're flat broke."

His jaw dropped open. Then he blustered, "What the heck are you talkin' about? I ain't broke—noways, I ain't."

"Oh, yeah? That's not what your ex-business manager, Kenneth Mayfield, told me. He said you've been putting a steady drain on your resources for a long time, and the well has run dry."

"That's a lie!"

He was about as convincing as a crooked politician at a congressional ethics hearing.

I was fast losing my patience. I jumped to my feet. "Freddie, I'm scared and I'm mad, and that's a very dangerous combination. I want you to cut all this garbage and tell me the truth. Here's what I think is going on, based on what I've learned the past few days. I think somebody had been blackmailing you, and I think it has been going on for quite some time. That's where all your money has been going. That's why you made those large monthly cash withdrawals from your bank account, which you wouldn't explain to your accountant. There's no other explanation."

The makeup was all that kept Freddie from turning white. He tried to back away from me, but I cornered him against a wall and accented my words with a finger poking him hard against his chest. "I think it all goes back somehow to that first recording you made with your original band, though I'll admit I can't figure out what you did that gave somebody the ammunition to blackmail you with. What was it, Freddie? What did you do that was so bad you were willing to keep paying and paying to shut somebody up? It's true-confession time, Freddie."

He stammered and blustered and looked scared. I could see I had about as much chance of prying the truth out of him at this point as I did of lifting the Empire State Building with a crowbar.

I moved away from him, pacing the room as I spoke my thoughts out loud, struggling to put the pieces of this crazy quilt together. "Let me see. When you first came to me, you were scared that somebody was trying to knock you off. You said somebody had been killing off the musicians from your first band, and you said some attempts had been made on your life. But it must not have been the blackmailer you were scared of. Why would the blackmailer want to kill you? That would be killing the goose that was laying the golden egg. No, I think that deep down you suspected it was Lorraine who was trying to do you in, though you hated to admit it to yourself because you were so crazy in love with her.

"I think Lorraine could have been somehow involved in the blackmail and that's why she got killed. Either she was in cahoots with the blackmailer and he killed her to keep from splitting the take, or she found out about it and threatened to blow the whistle on the blackmailer. The three musicians may have been killed because they knew who the blackmailer was, and he needed to shut them up."

I swung around to face him, my eyes blazing. "How about it, Freddie? Am I getting close?"

Obviously I was. He looked sick.

"How does Sam Tompkins figure in on all this? He bank-rolled your first recording, I found out. You never told me that, Freddie, among the other things you never told me. Tompkins is involved in a lot of things—your first recording, this Freddie Landers theme-park land deal. Is he involved in the blackmail?''

Freddie was having no more of it. He stumbled to the door, yanked it open, and called for his bodyguard.

At that point, it was leave or get thrown out, although as mad as I was, I don't think I would have stood for that. Freddie's bodyguard was a big, hard-bitten cowboy type who looked as if he could eat prickly-pear cactus, thorns and all, but I think I could have taken him. His type is usually stiff and muscle-bound. I probably could have thrown him through a window with a fast karate move. But I didn't see anything to be gained by breaking up the furniture at this point. I'd given Freddie plenty to think about. Maybe I'd shaken him up enough so that after a couple of days he'd decide to talk to me.

For now I'd just let him stew in his own juice.

I restrained an impulse to tell the bodyguard I thought his father rustled cattle and his mother made tamales out of dead coyotes, and I walked out. From the movie set, I drove to the office of Sam Tompkins. The fat, cigar-chomping wheeler-dealer was next on my list of persons to question, but his secretary informed me that he was not in his office today and she had no way of reaching him.

That was too bad, because Sam Tompkins was looking more and more like a key player in the real Freddie Landers story.

Frustrated, I drove to my office in Brownsville. The light on my telephone answering machine was blinking. I sat looking at it for a few minutes, working up the nerve to play back the message. I sure hoped it wasn't that computer voice again. Finally I drew a deep breath and punched the playback button.

The voice that came out of the machine was not the flat, mechanical sound of a computer. It was Crawfish Willie Atkins, sounding scared and desperate. "I need to talk to you right away," he said. "I got something important to tell you. Please come to my place as soon as you can."

I glanced at my watch. It was now ten o'clock. I had no idea when the message was phoned in. My machine isn't sophisticated enough to give the time calls are recorded. He might have called ten minutes ago or sometime last night. In any case, I wasted no time in locking up the office and driving to the shabby neighborhood where Willie lived.

I walked up the stairs and knocked at his door. There was no answer. I began to have that spooky feeling I had experienced the previous night. Same cold feeling of dread in the pit of my stomach, same prickly sensation at the back of my neck.

I tried the door. It was not locked. It swung inward a few inches. I called again. No answer.

It was dark inside. The feeling of dread was growing stronger, like an icy cold draft seeping from inside the apartment.

I tried to cross the threshold, but a primitive fear held me back. I tried to reason away my fear. When that didn't work, I went back to the truck, loaded Charlie's shotgun, and went back to the apartment with the gun cradled under my arm. I cocked the two hammers, kicked the door open, and strode into the apartment.

All the shades were drawn. It took a couple of moments for my eyes to adjust to the gloom. Then I saw Willie Atkins's body hanging from the rope around his neck.

Chapter Thirteen

I stood very still for a few long, cold moments. Then my shaky legs gave way and I sank onto the edge of the bed.

This was not the first dead body I had seen. That didn't make it any easier. I swallowed hard to keep the greasy lump in my stomach from crawling up my throat.

The object dangling from the rope could hardly be reconciled with the man I had shared a beer with in the Stardust Lounge last night. I closed my eyes, shutting out the sight of the hanging body for a moment, drew a shuddering breath, and tried to get some semblance of rational thought processes working.

I pried my eyes open, forcing myself to look at the remains of poor Crawfish Willie Atkins. The rope was tied to a light fixture. A chair was lying on its side underneath him as if he'd stood on it and then kicked it away. His feet were dangling a short distance above the floor, as if he could almost, but not quite, have reached it by standing on tiptoes.

Suicide? That was what it was meant to look like. I didn't

believe it for one second. That urgent phone message from Willie Atkins wanting to talk to me made this staged suicide a lie. He wanted to tell me something that might have identified the killer. The murderer got here first and did this.

I thought about last night in the bar, Willie glancing at the doorway, seeing something or someone that had spooked him into running home. I remembered the car driving away from in front of the bar. Somebody had been following me yesterday. That person had trailed me to that bar, had seen Willie talking to me, and decided he had to be eliminated before he talked too much.

With that realization came a wave of crushing guilt. I had led the killer to poor Willie. It was because he'd talked to me that he was now hanging by the neck, dead.

I pressed my palms against my burning eyes. Willie Atkins was a harmless little guy, just a third-rate fiddle player, who'd found life too puzzling and overwhelming to deal with, so he'd found refuge in the comforting numbness of booze and drugs. But he'd never hurt anybody, and he must have once had dreams and plans. Now, because of me, he was dead.

The sobering thought then came that the killing wasn't going to stop with Willie. Now Kate McHaney was the target. I'd poked into too many places, had asked too many questions. The killer simply could not rest easy until this meddling female private eye was as dead as Willie Atkins.

The instinct of self-preservation shook off the blue funk I was in and got me moving again.

I looked around the place. It was plain and shabby. The flowered pattern of the linoleum was worn away over the ridges of the floorboards. The wallpaper was streaked. The ceiling had brown-fringed circles where the roof leaked.

The furniture was early garage sale. The place smelled of mold, sweaty clothes, and stale beer.

Okay, now you call the police, I told myself. I would have a bit of explaining about how I happened to come there and find the body. There would be considerably more explaining to do if the police came and I was sitting there with a loaded shotgun. I removed that complication by unloading the gun and taking it back down to my truck. Then I returned to the apartment with a pair of cotton gloves I carried with the other junk piled behind the seat.

I decided it would not matter to Crawfish, and it would be only a minor obstruction of justice, if I nosed around the place a few minutes before dialing 911. I put on the gloves to avoid leaving fingerprints. I was also careful not to smear any that might already be there.

In a closet, I found Atkins's wardrobe, consisting of a couple of shirts and jeans and a hat, all needing cleaning. The bathroom medicine cabinet was filled with bottles that had prescription labels. There was a razor and soap and a few soiled towels. No drug paraphernalia that I could find. It looked as if, except for a few beers, Crawfish had been staying clean since his last drying-out.

In a dresser drawer there were a few pathetic personal possessions—a billfold with less than twenty dollars in it; some letters from his mother, who lived in San Antonio; a pocket knife; a key chain; comb; rubber bands; coiled violin strings in plastic bags; a couple of pencils; and a ballpoint pen. There was a small box with some personal memorabilia consisting of faded newspaper clippings advertising bands and dances where he'd played, quite a few unpaid bills and pawnshop tickets, and some snapshots. I recognized Willie's sister-in-law and her baby in some of the pictures.

Other pictures had been taken of Crawfish with different girls. Apparently, when he was younger, before the ravages of booze and drugs, he'd been reasonably good-looking and something of a ladies' man.

There were a number of pictures of Atkins with various country-western groups. One caught my eye. He was standing with a group in front of a building that bore the sign *Milt's Recording Studio*. It was obviously an earlier location than the building that currently housed Milton Bowman's recording business. Besides Crawfish, I recognized three other people in the group: Jimmy Joy Jamison and Freddie and Tammie Sue Landers. Freddie had his arm around Tammie Sue. It must have been taken when they were still married. I assumed that the other three people in the photograph, whom I did not recognize, were the three musicians who had died or been murdered in the last year.

There was a date on the back of the picture. I wondered if it had been taken at the time they made that fateful recording of "Remember Our Yesterdays." I supposed Tammy Sue, Freddie, or Jimmy Joy would know.

There was something about the picture that bothered me. I couldn't put my finger on what it was. But I stuck it in my pocket anyway. So I'd just added concealing evidence to my sins. Well, what the heck. I doubted if the picture would help the police much. They were probably going to call this a suicide.

I then picked up the phone. The police came very quickly. I spent the rest of the morning talking with a nice homicide detective, Lieutenant Alonzo Martinez, while technical people were busy around us, taking pictures, dusting for fingerprints, taking down the body, bagging it, and carrying it downstairs to the waiting ambulance. I had considerable explaining to do, but Lieutenant Martinez eventually accepted my explanation of how I happened to be the person who found Willie's body.

It was early afternoon before I finally was able to leave. I hadn't had lunch, but I wasn't hungry. After this morning's wrenching experience, food was the last thing on my mind. I was next on the killer's hit list. Mark Twain once said that when you know you're going to be hanged in the morning, it clears the mind wonderfully. I had no time to lose.

My next destination was the trailer park in Rio Dulce where Freddie's first wife lived. Remembering what had happened to Crawfish Willie Atkins, this time I made real certain I was not being followed.

On the way, I went over the theory I had been constructing.

I believed someone had been blackmailing Freddie. If I was right about that, it would explain several things—for example, why Freddie had been draining large amounts of cash every month from his resources until he was bled dry. It also tied Lorraine's murder into the situation.

A number of people I'd talked with had motives for murdering Lorraine—Sam Tompkins, who wanted her out of his land deal; Kenneth Mayfield, whom she had fired; even Freddie himself, who was in line to collect the insurance. But if my blackmail theory was correct, that was where the real motive lay.

Somebody had been blackmailing Freddie. Why? That was the big missing piece to the puzzle. It must have had something to do with the recording that brought fame to Freddie Landers. The musicians had been killed because they either knew the blackmailer or knew what he had that made Freddie pay him to keep quiet. Sam Tompkins had bankrolled the recording. That involved him. Lorraine had probably been killed by the blackmailer, either because she was involved in the scheme, or because she threatened to expose the blackmailer.

What about the one-armed man who had been a jump ahead of me when I was investigating Lorraine's past, and who recently had been nosing around asking Catfish Charlie and other waterfront characters about me? He was the wild card in the deck. I couldn't fit him in anywhere.

It was late afternoon when I arrived at Tammie Sue's mobile home. She had probably been up since noon and had by now gotten in three or four hours of serious drinking. She was dressed in a skirt and blouse and had made a stab at applying makeup and combing her hair.

She looked at me through the screen door, squinting to get her eyes focused.

"Hello, Tammie Sue," I said. "Do you remember me?"

She struggled with that for a moment, then nodded vaguely. "Yeah; you were here a couple of weeks ago. You're some kind of reporter person."

"Well, not exactly. Can I come in?"

She had a cigarette in one hand and a drink in the other. That gave her a problem for a few seconds, but she figured it out by putting the cigarette between her lips, thus freeing one hand to unhook the screen door.

When I entered, the same incredible clutter met my eyes. Tammie Sue made room for me to sit on the couch by shoving a pile of papers and clothing onto the floor. Staring at me balefully, a large striped cat was curled in a nearby easy chair. From the miasma of odors in the place, I deduced that his sandbox had not been changed in quite some time.

"Want a drink?" Tammy Sue asked.

"No thanks."

She placed her drink on a table beside the easy chair, rested her cigarette in an ashtray, picked up the cat, and sat in the chair, holding the cat on her lap. Then she retrieved her drink and cigarette.

"Tammie Sue, I didn't exactly tell you the truth the other day when I said I was a reporter. The fact is, I am a private detective."

"Yeah?" She looked at me with interest. "Like Cagney and Lacey on TV?"

"Well, in a way. They're actually badge-carrying cops. I work on my own."

"I never met a private eye before. Why did you tell me you were a reporter?"

"Sorry if I wasn't honest with you. I needed information and I thought at the time that was the best way to go about getting it. People sometimes get uptight when I tell them I'm a detective. Some things have happened, though, that have changed everything, and I have to be truthful with you. I guess you heard that Freddie's wife, Lorraine, was killed."

Her eyes clouded. She swallowed a large gulp of her drink. "Yeah, I heard. I didn't have any use for her. Freddie made a fool of himself over her. But I'm sorry she got killed. That's terrible."

"Are you still involved with the movie company filming the story about Freddie?"

"Nah, they finished with me. I did a couple of songs with Freddie and his band. That was all they wanted. I got paid pretty good, though."

I got the impression she was bored and lonesome and

glad to have somebody to talk to. She wasn't going to be so glad when I gave her the next bit of information.

"Tammie Sue, I've got some bad news. You remember Crawfish Willie Atkins?"

"Sure. I know Willie real good. I worked with him on several bands. He's a pretty good fiddler."

"Well, I'm sorry to have to tell you this, but Willie is dead."

All the color drained from Tammie Sue's face, leaving a mask of bright red lipstick and blotched mascara. "Dead?" she whispered. "When?"

"Early this morning sometime."

She gulped her drink, draining the glass. It rattled against her teeth.

"It was an apparent suicide, but I think someone might have killed him and made it look like suicide."

She stared at me, her eyes two wide, dark blotches in her white face. She got up abruptly, spilling the cat from her lap, and threaded her way through the clutter to where her bottle of bourbon sat on the kitchen drainboard. She dumped a considerable amount in her glass, drained it, refilled the glass, and came back to her chair, where she sank down weakly. She lit a fresh cigarette with trembling hands. Then the tears came, making trails of mascara down her cheeks. "Billy Joe Turner, Addie Davis, Tommy Mason," she intoned. "Now poor little Willie Atkins."

I took out the picture I'd found in Atkins's dresser drawer. "Do you remember this picture, Tammie Sue?"

She blew her nose on some tissues, wiped her eyes, and looked at the picture. She nodded. "Sure, that was me and Freddie and the band outside Milt's recording studio."

"Do you remember when it was made?"

She nodded. "Yeah, that was the day we recorded the album, the one with 'Remember Our Yesterdays.' After we finished recording, we went outside and Freddie had somebody take our picture. I think I've got a copy around here somewhere."

She stared at the picture, her eyes filling with tears. "They were all alive then. Now there's just me and Jimmy Joy and that bum, Freddie. Why couldn't it have been him instead of poor Willie?"

"You say you have a copy of this picture. Do you have anything else relating to the days when you were married to Freddie and singing in his band—any pictures, newspaper clippings, letters, things like that?"

I really didn't know what I was looking for. I was poking around, grasping for straws. The picture troubled me. There was something about it that had meaning if I could put my finger on it. Maybe Tammie Sue had something else that would give me a clue about what happened at that recording date.

She said, "Yeah, there's a box of stuff around here somewhere. I never throw anything away."

I could believe that.

"Tammie Sue, I'm trying to find out who has killed your musician friends and why. As long as the killer is running around loose, none of us is safe, and that includes me. He could be after you too. I need to dig up all the information I can, especially about those early days when Freddie was leading his first band and when all of you made that first recording."

She went into the bedroom and rummaged around for some time. Eventually she returned with a cardboard box crammed with junk. "I don't know if there's anything here that can help you. It's some stuff Freddie left when he moved out.''

We poked around in the box. There were yellowed newspaper clippings about Freddie's early success when his recording caught on, some old booking contracts, a few letters, several cassette tape recordings, pictures. All of it was covered with a film of dust that made me sneeze.

I found several snapshots of Freddie with his first band. One of them was a duplicate of the one I'd found in Willie Atkins's room, the band in front of the recording studio after cutting their album. Seeing it gave me that bothersome feeling again. I stared at it, wondering what it was about the scene that nagged me.

Tammie Sue was looking through the newspaper clippings, giggling when she found her name mentioned favorably in connection with the vocals on Freddie's record album.

''What are these cassette recordings?'' I asked.

She gathered them up, flipping them over one by one to read the labels. ''It's stuff Freddie recorded. Here's one of the band rehearsing. This is a jam session we had one night. This is one he made of his cousin Jeffrey playing his instruments. This one he made when we had a party here. He just turned on the recorder and let it run. Everybody was drunk.'' She chuckled at the memory.

I noticed that the cassettes were all labeled and dated. Tammie Sue tossed them back into the box and picked up a bundle of letters. ''These are fan letters Freddie started getting after the album came out. Boy, did they give him the swelled head. All of a sudden, he was getting famous. He changed after that,'' she said bitterly. ''I wasn't good enough for him anymore.''

"Do you know if there are any papers in here that have anything to do with the deal Freddie made with Sam Tompkins for Tompkins to finance that first recording?"

"Could be. I don't know what all's in here."

"Would you let me take this box home with me tonight? I really need to take the time to look at everything in here. I'll take care of it and get it back to you."

"Sure; I don't mind. Help yourself." She looked at me with apprehension-filled eyes. "I hope you find something."

I piled the box in my truck. It was dark by the time I got back to Brownsville. I stopped at my office. I was beginning to dread checking my answering machine, but this time the only call was from Steve. For a guy who didn't want any emotional ties, he was awfully persistent.

I'd lost my cassette deck in the houseboat fire, but I had a small, portable cassette player in the office. I took that with me and locked the office.

Then I headed straight for Charlie's waterfront café. I hadn't had a bite to eat all day. I was starting to feel pretty shaky. Charlie brought me a steaming platter of broiled flounder and hush puppies, which I wolfed down. I finished the meal with apple pie à la mode and drank two cups of coffee because I planned to stay up late.

I decided I'd better try Steve again. If he didn't hear from me, he'd probably figure out that I was up to something.

"Hi. It's me, Kate," I said when he answered the phone.

"Kate! Where have you been the past two days? I've been trying to reach you."

"Just pulling myself together," I lied. "I lost everything

in the fire. I had to go out and get new clothes and stuff.''
Well, that much was true, at least.

"Are you okay?'' He really sounded worried.

"As well as can be expected, I guess. I'll get over it.''

"You should have called me,'' he scolded. I hated to
admit it, but I kind of liked the protective tone in his voice.
So much for being a tough lady PI.

"As I recall, you wanted to cool things off for a while,''
I reminded him.

"I know what I said, Kate, but. . . .'' His voice trailed
off. "Look, can I come over? I think we need to talk.''

That certainly caught my interest. Could he be having a
change of heart? I was about to tell him to come on over
when I remembered the stuff I'd brought over from Tammie
Sue's place. Steve would hit the roof if he knew what I was
doing.

"Um, could it wait until tomorrow? I'm really pooped.''
I crossed my fingers and hoped he'd buy it.

"Okay. Tomorrow morning?''

"Better make it tomorrow night. I've really let my work
slide the past two days.''

"All right. And, uh, Kate?''

"Yes?''

"Never mind. I'll see you tomorrow.'' And on that cryp-
tic note, he hung up.

In my temporary quarters, Charlie's garage apartment, I
jammed a chair against the doorknob, loaded the shotgun
and propped it beside the bed, then dumped on the floor all
of the contents of Tammie Sue's junk box. I stuck one of
the cassettes into the tape player and let it play while I began
a careful study of each item from the box.

At one o'clock that night, my ears were throbbing from listening to four hours of tape recordings, my back was aching, and my eyes were burning, but now I was pretty sure I knew why Freddie Landers was being blackmailed. And I was very close to identifying the killer.

Chapter Fourteen

E verything led back to that first recording, "Remember Our Yesterdays."
The next morning I drove to Greensborough, where the
recording had been made. I spent most of the morning in
the courthouse, going through records. At noon, I stopped
to have a sandwich and a Coke. Then I stopped in at an
electronics store to have a copy made of one of the cassette
tapes I had listened to last night. I asked some questions
there and also at music stores around town.

Then I drove around for a while, hunting an address. I
found it near the outskirts of town in a neighborhood of
used-car lots, Laundromats, bars, thrift shops, and vacant
lots. The buildings were seedy; many needed paint, and
quite a few were empty, with plywood covering broken
glass. I drove along slowly, checking addresses until I came
to the storefront I was looking for. I pulled up at the curb,
making sure I was at the right place. After looking at it for
a while, I drove away and returned to Brownsville.

I stopped at a shopping center. At a discount clothing

167

store, I bought a pair of black jeans, a black T-shirt, and a black scarf. There wasn't much more I could do until nightfall, so I went back to my office and spent the afternoon taking care of paperwork.

At sundown, I drove to my garage apartment and changed into the black jeans and T-shirt. Then I went down to the waterfront, to Charlie's café. All my senses were on high alert. My stomach felt tight, my nerves jittery. I was too keyed up to eat. But I had to see Charlie before I left.

His jukebox was playing Artie Shaw's theme song, "Nightmare," an apt enough selection for the hours ahead. Charlie came over to my table with a menu, but I told him I just wanted coffee tonight. He ran knobby fingers through his shock of white hair, giving me a hard look. "You're dressed like you're about to do some breaking and entering."

You're a perceptive old coot, I thought. "Charlie, would you do me a favor? Call Steve Gannon for me in about"— I glanced at my watch—"two hours. Tell him I'd like for him to drive over and meet me in Greensborough."

"What's in Greensborough?"

"That's where it all started, where Freddie Landers recorded 'Remember Our Yesterdays.' I think I'm on to something."

Charlie looked worried. "Kid, are you going to do something crazy?"

"No, I think I'm going to do something smart. If I'm right, I'll have some pretty solid evidence. I may even hand Steve the name of Lorraine's killer."

"Sounds dangerous to me," he grumbled. "Why don't you talk to Steve now?"

"Because I don't have any proof, but I think I can get it tonight."

"And maybe get yourself killed doing it?" he said, his wrinkled, weather-beaten face drawn up in a dark scowl. "Maybe I'd better go with you."

"Not a chance. You stay here and call Steve, like I told you."

"Where in Greensborough is he supposed to meet you?"

"Well, I guess in front of the courthouse at the town square is as good a place as any. He can go with me from there to make the arrest if I'm right."

I drank the coffee and left. It would be a lonely night drive. I wanted to take Bismark with me for company, but discarded that idea, knowing he'd just get in the way.

It took me about an hour to drive to Milt's Recording Studio in Greensborough. If my timing was right, and if I was lucky, I should be able to do my job in an hour and be ready to meet Steve at the courthouse.

The recording studio was dark, a fact that didn't surprise me. The front area of the parking lot was illuminated by streetlights, but the lot in back of the building was in darkness. That was where I parked my truck, hidden in deep shadows beside a cluster of banana trees.

I sat there for a moment with the window rolled down. It was very quiet here.

From behind the seat, I took a small satchel. In it were a flashlight and some tools.

I tied the black scarf around my hair, then I stepped out of the truck, eased the door closed, and melted into the shadows. My target was a rear window.

Fortunately, Bowman did not have burglar bars on the building. I got out the small flashlight and, holding it between my teeth, I searched the bag for a knife and glass cutter. First I used a knife to cut the screen. Then I spit on a rubber suction cup and fastened it near the bottom of the pane, scored a circle in the glass, tapped it until the scored line broke, then lifted free the part I'd cut out, which was stuck to the suction cup.

That part was easy. I shone the light around the inside of the aluminum window frame and saw the alarm system attached to the window frame. It was simple but effective. If the window was lifted, contact was broken and all kinds of alarms and lights went off like a pinball machine flashing ''tilt!''

I had to do some more glass cutting, which took time. I cut the glass out all the way around the frame. It helps to be somewhat handy with tools if you're in the private-investigating business. When I was through, I had room to crawl through the frame without raising it and without cutting myself on any glass. I put the bag of tools back in the truck and took the shotgun down from the headache rack and loaded it. I carried it back with me and carefully lowered it through first, propping it against the wall beside the window. Then I crawled through the narrow opening, glad that I was on the small side.

Inside Milt's recording studio, I snapped on my flashlight. I found myself in one of the recording rooms. The walls were insulated. There were numerous microphones, music stands, and a piano. One wall was mostly plate glass. Behind it was the control booth with a lot of recording equipment and control panels.

I left through a doorway and found myself in the hall. My goal was Milt's office. Once I was in there, I searched his desk and filing cabinets. What I was after was his books.

When I located them, I spread them out on his desk, flipped on a small desk lamp, and began perusing the columns of figures.

If there was any sound when the front door opened, I didn't hear it. Maybe I was too absorbed in my task. I was caught completely by surprise when the room was flooded with light. I straightened up abruptly with a gasp.

Cousin Milton was standing in the doorway pointing a nasty little pistol at me. He was well turned out as usual in black-and-white shoes, sharply creased slacks, a maroon silk shirt, and a blood-red bow tie. For once he was not wearing a sport coat. There were dark circles of perspiration around the armpits of his shirt and little beads of sweat standing out on his forehead.

From behind him in the hallway, I heard his wife's querulous voice. "Who is it, Milt?"

"Why, it's Kate McHaney, dear."

"The detective lady that said she was a relative at Freddie's party?" Elaine asked.

"Yes," Milt said, looking at me intently, his finger pressing dangerously tight on the trigger of his pistol.

His wife asked fretfully, "How'd she get in here, anyway?"

"I was about to ask her. How'd you get in, Miss McHaney?" His eyes were glassy and bulging in his plump, round, perspiring face.

I moved slowly away from the desk, feeling cold all over. If you want to have your life pass before your eyes, try looking down the business end of a nasty little revolver held by a nervous, trigger-happy killer. It took considerable effort, but I somehow kept my voice steady and soothing.

"Cousin Milt, why don't you point that gun somewhere else? You don't need a gun."

"Don't I?" he asked.

"You couldn't shoot me. How could you explain shooting me?"

"Oh, that would be easy. We were driving by, saw a light in my office, went in, heard someone moving around. I thought you were a burglar, and I shot. A jury would believe that."

"The way they believed Crawfish Willie Atkins hanged himself? The way Billy Joe Turner was killed by a hit-and-run driver, Addie Davis was knifed by a mugger, and Tommy Mason set his bed on fire with a cigarette?"

"Why, I don't know what you're talkin' about," he said blandly, his face growing shinier with sweat. He did not move the pistol.

"Sure you do," I said. I took a cassette tape out of my pocket. "Play this and you'll hear how I know what I'm talking about."

I tossed the unlabeled cassette to him. He caught it with his free hand. "What is this?"

"It's a copy I made this morning of the original. Want to hear what's on it?"

"Tell me."

"I think it would be better if you heard it."

It was a play for time. Milton probably knew that, but his curiosity about the tape got the better of his judgment.

He scowled at the tape and at me. Then he waved the gun at me. "Come on."

He backed away, keeping the gun pointed at me. I walked slowly into the hallway.

I saw Elaine standing in the hallway, looking distressed,

one plump hand pressed against her cheek. The thick red lipstick on her Cupid's-bow lips was slightly smeared. "Miss McHaney," she said, "you're a bad person, breaking in here like this."

"I know," I agreed.

Milt handed the cassette tape to his wife. "Would you please put this on the machine in the control room, dear?"

Her bracelets jangled as she accepted the tape.

We traipsed back to the studio room where I had made my entrance into the building. Milton switched on the overhead fluorescents, looked at the window I had cut open, shook his head, and went, "Tsk . . . tsk . . . tsk. The police are going to find your fingerprints all over that window after I tell them how you broke into my studio and I had to shoot you."

"I wouldn't be surprised," I said, glancing at the shotgun propped near the window and measuring my chances at reaching it before Milton shot me full of holes.

"Sit," he commanded.

We took our seats in folding chairs in the studio room. Behind the plate glass in the control room, Elaine snapped the cassette into the equipment, turned some dials, and punched a button.

The studio room was filled with the piano music of Jeffrey Stovall, Freddie's young, mentally handicapped cousin. The music was much in the style I had heard Jeffrey play the day I visited Roy Stovall's ranch house. On the tape, Jeffrey was obviously improvising, playing snatches of melodies as they raced through his mind. There were no complete songs, only fragments of haunting, lovely themes welling up from a strange spark of genius hidden deep within his being.

"Recognize who's playing, Cousin Milton?" I asked.

"Why, yes," he said softly, smiling at me. His glassy, bulging eyes had a chilling expression. "That there is little Jeffrey playing his music the way he plays, kind of making it up as he goes along."

"Do you remember when the tape was made?"

"I think I do. Freddie brought the boy around one day and asked if I'd let him play on the piano and make a tape of him playing."

"That was a number of years ago," I said. "The original tape had a date on it. It was made back when you had that dinky little storefront recording studio over on Redondo Street."

"I believe it was," Milton said, looking at me carefully.

"That was before Freddie wrote 'Remember Our Yesterdays,' before he became famous, and before you got rich, Milton. That was before you had this modern, sophisticated recording studio, before you were driving a Cadillac, and living in that expensive home you moved into last year."

"You know an awful lot about my personal life, Miss McHaney."

"I spent some time at the courthouse this morning, finding out about the property you've acquired since Freddie became famous. Quite impressive. Not long after Freddie began raking in the big bucks, you took out permits to have this building constructed. Last year, you bought some expensive residential property where you and Elaine now live. It's all in the courthouse records. I saw a picture of Freddie and his band taken in front of that pitiful little storefront recording studio you ran before Freddie became famous. Something about that picture kept bothering me. This morning I drove to the poor neighborhood where your original studio was located, and I finally realized what it was that bothered me. How could you possibly go from operating such a measly little business to owning an expensive building like this and driving a Cadillac in such a short time? How did you get all that money, Milton?''

"Made it out of Freddie's hit record and with my recording business.''

"No, you didn't. You were too cheap to give the financial backing for your cousin's album. Sam Tompkins financed Freddie's first recording. He was the one who made the profit from the record sales of that hit. The only thing you got out of it was what you made from cutting the records— not nearly enough to explain how you went from a little hole-in-the-wall recording business to all this opulence.

"And your recording business isn't all that great. I asked around at music stores. Your recording studio is something of a local joke. The music stores tell me you do a little recording for church groups and Mexican *conjunto* bands. I confirmed that when I looked at your books tonight. This recording studio is just a front, Milton. You've been getting your money from your cousin Freddie. You've bled him dry to pay you to keep quiet about who really wrote all his hit songs. Freddie never wrote 'Remember Our Yesterdays,' 'Your Head on My Pillow,' 'Long Gone from Here,' or any of the songs he claims to have written. He got the themes of all of them from his cousin Jeffrey. He heard Jeffrey improvising those lovely themes when the boy sat at the piano. Freddie put Jeffrey's improvisations into commercial form, gave them a title and words, and became famous. You knew who the real composer was. If you exposed Freddie, it would ruin him.''

Milton said sourly, "Freddie is just a dumb country boy

with very little talent. He looks good in front of a band and he can sing a little. That's about all. He doesn't deserve all that money. I got every bit as much right to it as he has.''

"I guess you had to do away with the members of the original band because they suspected Freddie couldn't have written those songs. They probably guessed he got the melodies from his cousin. Maybe they were even starting rumors about Freddie being an impostor and you had to shut them up before they ruined your source of income. Weren't you concerned about Jeffrey's father?''

Milton shrugged. "Roy Stovall's got a tin ear. He hasn't got the musical ear or sense enough to figure out that Freddie stole the melodies from Jeffrey. Freddie buys instruments for Jeffrey and gives them some money every month. That's all Uncle Roy cares about.''

I had to keep playing for time. My only chance was to keep him talking. "But why did you strangle Lorraine?''

Now that we'd broken the ice, he didn't seem to mind telling me. Maybe it helped to get it off his chest.

"Lorraine was going to kill the goose that was laying the golden eggs. I suspected from the beginning that she had married Freddie to get his money. I really started getting worried when Lorraine had Freddie take out the million-dollar life-insurance policy. I suspected Lorraine's first attempt on Freddie was the food poisoning, and the second was when he nearly got electrocuted. The next time she'd probably have succeeded. With Freddie dead, it wouldn't matter if Freddie's plagiarism was exposed.

"I tried to warn Freddie, but Freddie wouldn't listen. Freddie was too much in love with Lorraine to have good sense, but I guess I must have planted some seeds of doubt and that was why Freddie hired you to check out Lorraine.''

He went on, "I'd already hired my own private detective from an agency in San Antonio to find out who Lorraine really was."

"Ah!" I exclaimed. "That was the mysterious one-armed man who stayed one jump ahead of me. He was your private detective. You also had him checking on me."

Milton nodded. "And when I found out about Lorraine's lurid past, I knew I had to eliminate Lorraine."

"Why didn't you just tell Freddie what you found out about Lorraine?"

"I was afraid it wouldn't do any good. She had Freddie wrapped around her little finger. And there was no proof she knocked off her first two husbands. One was cremated, the other burned up in his car. She might have sweet-talked Freddie into believing she was innocent—convinced him that it was all just a tragic coincidence—and that poor sap would have believed her. But I really had a more urgent reason than that. More and more Lorraine was taking over Freddie's business and private affairs. She found out about my little financial arrangement with Freddie. She couldn't stand the thought of somebody milking money out of Freddie that she wanted. She was cold-blooded enough to hire a hit man to kill me. I expected her to have a contract out on me anytime. So it had gotten down to the point of who killed who first."

"Wasn't it kind of dumb, strangling her with Freddie's belt?" I asked.

"That was a mistake," Milton admitted. "I just grabbed the first thing that was handy to strangle her with, and it happened to be one of Freddie's belts. But I figured there was no way the police could definitely tie him to the murder. Freddie was fifty miles away, being filmed by the movie company. That seemed like the perfect alibi to protect Freddie. I didn't dream Freddie's alibi would have a hole in it because at the time of the murder, Freddie was not on the movie set and could conceivably have driven home and returned without being missed. Still, that's a very weak case. There were no witnesses to place Freddie at the house when Lorraine died. So I'm not worried that they'll prosecute Freddie. The state doesn't have a strong enough case to indict him.''

Milton was tired of talking. He stood up, his expression becoming more intense, his hand gripping the gun tighter. I thought, *Kate McHaney, it's now or never.*

I stood up too, my right hand on the back of the folding chair. I suddenly tightened my grip and swung the chair at Cousin Milton with all my strength; at the same time, I threw myself at the wall where Charlie's shotgun was propped.

Everything happened at once. The chair hit Milton at the same time that his gun went off. Over the loudspeaker came Elaine's piping screech. I grabbed the shotgun. It was pointed toward the ceiling. I didn't have time to aim. I just pulled the trigger and hoped I'd hit something. When that thing went off, it sounded like a whole battery of field artillery. There was a great flash of fire and smoke. As I'd suspected, the thing kicked like a mule. The charge of buckshot ripped out the whole section of the ceiling that contained the fluorescent light fixture.

The room was plunged into darkness. The little cannon had kicked me against the wall. My ears were ringing and deafened from the blast. Faintly I heard Elaine screeching over and over. I cocked the other hammer, braced myself against the wall, and fired blindly. I heard a great shattering of glass and I guessed I'd taken out the control room. I hoped Elaine had gotten out of there first. If not, she was hamburger.

I heard feet running down the hall, heard doors slam.

I got up, fell over a tangle of music stands, got up again, and crawled out of the window in an undignified hurry.

The next thing I was in my truck, glad to be alive, and pulling around to the front of the building. I got there in time to see Cousin Milt's Cadillac taking off with Milt behind the wheel. Elaine was beside him. She looked right at me through the window as they whipped past. Her hair was a mess and her lipstick was smeared all over her face.

At the same time, I saw a sheriff's cruiser coming down the street. As Cousin Milt's Cadillac went bouncing out of the parking lot and down the street with screeching tires, the flashing lights went on in the sheriff's cruiser. As he went into hot pursuit, I saw Steve behind the wheel.

"Go get him, baby," I said. Suddenly I became aware of blood running down my sleeve. I put my head down on my steering wheel.

Things began swimming around. Something turned all the lights off. I seemed to float in and out of the blackness. Whenever the lights came back on, I was aware of a gigantic pain in my left shoulder. Once when I drifted out of the dark haze, I was aware of strong arms lifting me out of the truck. I looked up into Steve's beautiful, rugged face.

I heard myself say, "Hi," weakly. My voice was coming from a long way off.

"Don't talk," he said.

But I kept looking at his wonderful face. I heard myself

say, "I love you." I don't know why I said it out loud. At that point I couldn't be held responsible for my actions.

"I know," he said. "Now be quiet. The ambulance is coming."

He was looking at me with a strange, worried expression. There were tears in his eyes. Tears in the eyes of tough, John Wayne-type Steve Gannon? Nah. I had to be hallucinating.

I started going bye-bye again. I made an effort to get things back in focus. My shoulder was having the granddaddy of all pains. I whispered, "Cousin Milt . . . Elaine . . . ?"

"They're in the backseat of my cruiser, handcuffed. Now here's the ambulance."

That was about it for a while. Then I kind of remember being in the ambulance and feeling Steve's big hand holding mine tightly. It was a good feeling.

Epilogue

At the hospital, they called in a surgeon to take the slug out of my shoulder. I was put under a general anesthetic, so I was checked out of events for the rest of that night, and the next day I was so full of sedatives and pain killers I didn't know who I was—or care.

Toward evening, my mind did begin functioning, something which was good because that was when Steve came quietly into the room, carrying a huge bunch of roses. It was the first time anybody ever gave me a lot of roses like that. I thought, *Gee, it was worth getting shot for this.*

Steve sat beside my bed for a long time. We didn't talk much. They had me so doped up, it was one of the few times in my life that my tongue wouldn't operate, which was just as well. I sensed a feeling between us that words would have spoiled.

When there was any talking, Steve did most of it. He said in a kind of gruff voice, ''You're going to be fine,

Kate. I talked to the doctor. You'll have a bum arm for a while, but no permanent damage.''

He was looking at me in that peculiar way and his eyes were damp. This time I knew I wasn't hallucinating. Those *were* tears in the eyes of that big, he-man Western-type lawman. Tears for me. How about that?

Steve tried to be severe when he shook his head and muttered, ''I don't know what I'm going to do with you, McHaney. Breaking into the recording studio. Having a shoot-out with Milton Bowman. You could have gotten yourself killed.''

I tried to look contrite, but I was enjoying the look of caring concern in Steve's eyes too much.

He explained that it was not entirely a lucky coincidence that he happened by the recording studio just as Milton was pulling out. When Catfish Charlie called Steve to tell him to meet me in Greensborough at the courthouse, he also told Steve what I'd said about Greensborough being where it all started—where Freddie Landers recorded 'Remember Our Yesterdays.' Steve put two and two together and suspected that I'd be going to the recording studio, so he headed straight there instead of the courthouse. Luckily he arrived just as Milton and Elaine were speeding away.

A few weeks later, a grand jury indicted Milton Bowman for the murder of Lorraine Landers. The prosecutor has a pretty strong case. In addition to my testimony, the Landers's maid has identified Milton as the man she saw dragging Lorraine out to his car the morning she was murdered. Freddie Landers has also come forward and admitted that Milton has been blackmailing him ever since his recordings became a hit. So, in addition to the murder charge, Milton Bowman has been indicted for blackmail and extortion. One way or the other he is going to be put away for a long, long time.

Unfortunately, it will be hard to prove Milton had anything to do with the deaths of the musicians. I'm sure it was Milton who set fire to my houseboat, but arson is hard to prove.

As for the drugged coffee that almost caused me to have a wreck after Freddie's party, we're convinced it was Lorraine who was responsible for that. Freddie's bodyguard admitted that Lorraine paid him to follow me in the Bronco and attempt to run me off the road that night when the drugged coffee made me groggy.

Freddie's confession of plagiarizing his melodies of course set off a scandal that rocked the entertainment world. On national television, *20/20* did a piece about the scandal, and Freddie's downfall was a lead story on the cover of the *National Enquirer*. Freddie's career in the national limelight was ended. The movie company that had been doing his life story packed up and went home. Sam Tompkins's Freddie Landers theme-park real-estate venture went down the tubes. But Freddie was not left destitute. He collected the million-dollar life-insurance benefit from Lorraine's death, so he can continue his life-style. He's put together a small country-western band and is playing for local dances.

I'm having trouble collecting my fee from Freddie for discovering Lorraine's murderer. Freddie isn't too happy that in the process of finding Lorraine's murderer, I also brought about his public disgrace and downfall. I may have to sue.

My landlord found a suitable barge and built another houseboat for me to live on.

After I got settled in my new home, I invited Steve over

for a housewarming. It was a lovely night, with a full moon sparkling on the water. We had a candlelight dinner. I served broiled steak, baked potatoes, and Steve's favorite, avocado salad.

After dinner, we sat on the deck under the stars. I'd borrowed a record of romantic Glenn Miller melodies from Catfish Charlie. It was playing softly on my new stereo. Steve and I sat there, all mellowed out from the food, the wine, the moonlight, and the music. We held hands. Steve kissed me. I kissed him back.

We did that a lot.

Somewhere, after a while, when we came up for breath, Steve said, "McHaney, I'm getting my head straight about us. You know, I was pretty shell-shocked after the breakup of my marriage. I guess I was gun-shy. I swore I wasn't going to get involved again. You came along and knocked my guard down. I tried not to care about you, but I did . . . a lot . . . I mean I do . . . well, I guess you know what I mean—"

The way he was looking at me, I guess I did.

Looks like my luck with men has finally changed.